ENTER

Superintendent Flagg

JOHN CASSELLS

JOHN LONG

London

JOHN LONG LIMITED

178–202 Great Portland Street, London, W.1

AN IMPRINT OF THE HUTCHINSON GROUP

London Melbourne Sydney
Auckland Bombay Toronto
Johannesburg New York

First published 1959

This book has been set in Times New Roman type face. It has been printed in Great Britain by The Anchor Press, Ltd., in Tiptree, Essex, on Antique Wove paper and bound by Taylor Garnett Evans & Co., Ltd., in Watford, Herts

1

IT IS a well-known aphorism that the best of men make the worst mistakes, a truism to which Superintendent Flagg was completely devoted. Flagg, himself, made few mistakes and when he did usually contrived with consummate success to have them pinned on someone else—a specious design, which Inspector Prosser would never for one moment have tolerated, had it even occurred to him. It most certainly never did occur to him. Inspector Prosser was a person of considerable standing in police circles, respected as a churchgoer and a man, a figure of reproach to lesser and more sinful policemen, of whom Flagg was one. In his way he was a good officer —years in advance of his times—and it is indubitably true that many of his ideas were received by his superiors and acted upon in the public interest with very little harm being done to anyone at all. There were other occasions, however, when one might not be too sure of Prosser's methods—or of their results. In the matter of Digby Branchman, C.A., Prosser's judgement was appallingly at fault, though it took all of twenty years to make this fact clear. And yet, as Flagg sententiously decreed, 'Truth will out.' In this case it did, yet it was a pity that men had to die to disprove a theory.

In the eyes of the world at large, the name of Mark Bentley was associated with the various sporting proclivities which were so much his natural bent, but there was another and radically different side to his character and, if Jane Bentley knew him as an indulgent and good-natured father, Faith Bentley, herself, had to admit his virtues as a husband and as a provider of comfort and even luxury.

In proof of the comfort, there was the rarely occupied town flat in Grosvenor Square; and the cheerful, rambling country place at Marchgate Priory. Things had not always been just so advantageously contrived. There had been a time when a flat in Brockley had taxed their resources, but that had been a long time ago. So long a time that Faith had forgotten as much of it as was convenient—and that was quite a lot. But there were one or two things she had never forgotten and there were one or two people.

Tommy Osborne was one of the people. Tommy with his ready smile and his profligate charm. Sometimes the memory of him would come back to her, bitter sweet in its intensity. Sometimes she wondered where he was now —wondered whether he was alive or dead. There had been a story that he had died out in Toronto, but she no more than half believed it, though, oddly enough Mark, himself, thought it was true.

'Had it from Verrall,' he would say, when the matter came up for discussion, as it occasionally did. 'Tommy was mixed up in some sort of underhand business. I don't know what it was, but it was against the law. Anyway, the story is that he got himself shot. Verrall knew a man who knew . . .'

And so it went. Verrall was the sort of person who always knew a man who knew a man. A tall, stringy, hard-eyed man, yellow-skinned and dry as a walnut, he was Mark's lawyer, someone who paid them occasional visits and had done so over all the years of Faith's married life. She had never liked him overmuch, and it had annoyed her secretly that Mark should have accorded to this unpopular man his loyal support.

'Old Verrall? He's all right, Faith. One of the best.'

'But I don't like him,' she would protest. 'There's

6

something queer about him, Mark. Something underhand, don't you think? I feel he's ever so cunning.'

'He's a lawyer,' Mark would say comfortably. 'All lawyers are a bit underhand. You know that yourself, Faith. And as for being cunning, well, he wouldn't be much use unless he was. Not to me, anyway. Verrall's all right. He makes money for me. That's important.'

She was quite content to leave it at that, for if money was important to Mark, it was almost equally so to her. From then onwards, Verrall was tolerated, even cultivated a little at times, for she was still curious about Tommy and hoped for more specific information than had yet been supplied. And at length, when the appropriate occasion had arrived, she had put the question to him.

Verrall had been thoughtful. 'Tommy Osborne? Yes, of course I knew him. I can't say I knew him well. I only met him once or twice.'

She led the conversation round to Osborne's untimely demise and here Verrall was as positive as a man could well be. 'Osborne's dead. I had it from a police sergeant who knew all about it. He was shot, someplace up in northern Ontario—years ago it was. This friend of mine was in the district at the time, so you can rely on it.'

And yet she often thought of Tommy, picturing him as he had been in the early days of their marriage; in the days before Mark had come along, with his charm and his money. Tommy had given her the divorce when she had asked him. He'd been queerly dignified about it all— much more than she herself had been, much more even than she had deserved. Jane had been no more than a baby in arms in those days. She was twenty-two now— slim, tall, and with Tommy's grey eyes and more than a hint of Tommy's flashing temper. This tempestuous vitality she had always ascribed to his Scottish forbears,

7

but, had she attempted it, a sharper analysis might have provided a more reasonable explanation.

In point of fact, she was inclined to be an unreasonable woman, spoiled, petted, pampered, and more than a little neurotic. At forty she had the looks and the figure which had been hers at twenty, and for them made no obeisance to artifice. Mark Bentley frankly adored her. More than that, he understood her, and if, in his more contemplative moments, he recognized her frailties for what they were, he would not for worlds have changed them.

Jane was different. If she loved her mother she was under no illusions—nor did she even make the pretence of being so. Faith Bentley found her a disconcerting companion—at times even an alarming one, and in her moments of exasperation would confide mainly in Mark. 'It's the awful things she does, Mark,' she would say tearfully.

They rarely seemed so awful to Mark. 'What's she been up to now?' he would inquire lazily, and for an hour by the clock she would tell him. In the end these charming little domestic scenes usually ended with Mark taking her in his arms, kissing her and saying: 'There, now, Faith. Don't you worry any more about it. I'll have a word with Jane and we'll see what can be done.'

But nothing ever was done. Usually Mark forgot all about it, and even if he had remembered, in the face of Jane's opposition, his own good resolutions would very soon have bowed themselves out. The interesting affair of Peter Blane was a case in point. Faith sat in the comfort of the snug morning-room, her blue eyes intent on the flickering logs which filled the hearth. Then, after a moment or so, she turned them on Mark and in them there was both uneasiness and reproach. 'I'm so worried about it,' she said.

Mark Bentley looked over the top of his glasses at her. He was tall, fair, just a little bit florid, but still on the

8

right side of fifty. 'I don't think you need to be, Faith. She's twenty-two. When you were her age you were married, had a baby, were divorced and re-married. I shouldn't worry about Jane.'

'But I do. She's got no right to be friendly with a man like Blane. There are dozens of quite delightful people in the district and she has to spend all her time with a common barman.'

'He's not just that. After all, he owns the Knight Templar.'

'I suppose he does. But he works in the bar, doesn't he? Goodness knows what sort of language she'll pick up —not to mention ideas.'

Mark was a little startled. 'My dear girl, you're getting worked up about nothing at all. You've never even seen him.'

'I don't need to see him,' Faith said calmly. 'I can use my imagination. I've spoken to her about it before this and she just won't pay any attention to me. Mark, you've got to talk to her.'

Mark wriggled. 'It isn't easy to talk to Jane. You know what she's like. She just won't listen.'

'Jane's incorrigible.' She sighed as she thought of this wayward child. 'I can't understand her, Mark. But something has to be done. My nerves are troubling me again—palpitations.'

He was perturbed. 'When was this?'

'After dinner. You were out at the time. You'll speak to Jane for me, darling. Promise me you will.' She leaned towards him.

If there was one quality about Mark Bentley that was more genuine than any other, it was his affection for the pretty, neurotic little charmer who had enslaved him twenty years before. He came over, leaned down and kissed her. 'Of course I will. I'll speak to Blane.'

'Will that be any easier than speaking to Jane?'

'For me it will be.'

It was not quite what she had in mind. 'Suppose he doesn't listen to you?'

Mark put one hand under her chin. 'Don't you worry about anything like that. Blane is quite a good sort. He must be as old as I am. Get the idea out of your head that there's anything romantic in this friendship. I'm pretty sure he'll listen to me.'

'I hope so,' Faith listened, her head on one side. 'That sounds like Jane now, Mark. Do you want to speak to her now?'

'Not me,' Mark Bentley said cheerfully. He ruffled her hair and passed out of the doorway, hurrying his step so that he might at least turn the corner before Jane should make her appearance. He was successful, but only just. There were moments when even he could wish she were a shade more subtle in her approaches. Perhaps Faith was nearer to being right than she knew. A word with Blane might do no harm. He went softly along the hall, drew on a coat and lifted a heavy tweed cap. He walked along to the front door, had almost reached it when he heard the telephone ring. For a second he halted, then began to walk back. It was ringing in the study, which was along to his right. He reached it, then went in, lifted the receiver. 'This is Marchgate Close.'

A man's voice said: 'Why, so it is! And this is Mark Bentley listening, I'll be bound. Remember me, Mark?'

Mark licked his lips. 'Who's talking?'

There was no immediate answer. For a second or two he thought the caller had hung up, then he heard a soft laugh. 'Worried, Mark?'

'Not so much worried as curious. Who are you?'

'Try guessing. Try guessing, Mark. For all the good it will do you.'

Bentley said quietly: 'What's the idea? What's it all about?'

10

There was no answer. Mark went on softly: 'You've called up before. Twice before. That means you're leading up to something. What is it?'

There was a little ripple of laughter, then a sudden 'click'. The line went dead. Mark took the receiver away from his ear for a moment or two, looked at it, then laid it down. He stood for a moment or so, one hand on the desk, in an attitude of some considerable mystification, then pushed open the door and went into the corridor. Something moved at the end of it. He fancied he saw a shadow. Clancy, or one of the girls. Now he spoke sharply. 'Clancy. Are you there?'

There was no response. Then, to his ears came the soft shuffling of feet on stone steps. He hurried to the end of the corridor, switched on the cluster of lights which lit the rather wide entrance hall.

It was empty.

Puzzled and perplexed he pushed wide the big oak doorway. There was something peculiar here and Mark Bentley had no time for any mystery which was not of his own devising.

2

THE village of Marchgate Priory lay some two miles from the Close—a small and somewhat picturesque huddle of cottages clustering round a Norman church.

The Knight Templar commanded the bridge, its gardens sloping down to the brook itself, its boat-house and slip observable from the opposite bank in its neat green and white paintwork. Along one gable ran, like a fluttering banner, the designation:

THE HOSPITABLE HOUSE
Prop. : Peter Blane

Mark Bentley surveyed it soberly as he approached the bridge. It was all but dark now and one or two lights twinkled high up on the gable. Mark swung over the bridge, then down into the long courtyard which led round to the rear of the building. He was in the corridor when a trim, uniformed maid met him. 'Good afternoon, sir.'

Mark smiled. 'Isn't it? I want to see Mr. Blane if he's around.'

She looked dubious. 'Mr. Blane's in his office, but I don't know if he'll see you, sir. He doesn't like to be disturbed.'

'Disturb him,' Mark said. He grinned at her. 'The name is Bentley. Mr. Bentley from Marchgate Close.'

She was on the point of turning away when a new thought seemed to occur to her. 'Are you Miss Bentley's father?'

'I have that honour,' Mark said humorously. 'Will it make any difference?'

She thought it might. 'Miss Bentley comes here quite a lot.' She went away briskly enough, and Mark watched her, half amused, half irritated. She came back in a moment or so. 'Mr. Blane will see you, sir. You've to come through to the business-room.' She led the way up a narrow stairway and along an equally narrow corridor. At the end of it was a small oak door, on it a hand-printed sign which read:

STRICTLY PRIVATE

The girl tapped on the door, turned the handle. 'Mr. Bentley, sir.'

12

Mark stepped inside, closing the door behind him as he did so. Blane had been sitting at a large, old-fashioned desk. He rose now, a man of average height, clean-shaven and bronzed. 'Good afternoon, Mr. Bentley. Will you sit down?'

Mark sat down on one side of the wide and cheerful fire. 'You're jolly comfortable here, Blane.'

Peter Blane laughed. 'I like to think I am, Mr. Bentley.' He produced a decanter, glasses and a syphon. When he had attended to the requirements of his visitor, he poured out a drink for himself, then came over towards the fire. 'Now, Mr. Bentley. What can I do for you?'

Mark sipped at his drink, a little at a loss for a second. This was hardly the opening he had pictured. 'Damned good whisky, Blane. The best I've tasted for a long time. Where do you get it?'

'It's rather special,' Blane admitted. 'I get six bottles a year. I make no apologies for retaining it for my own personal consumption.'

Mark sampled some more of it in the hope that under its mellow and beneficent glow the problem which was uppermost in his mind might dissolve itself away. 'I hope I'm not disturbing you, old boy. I'm rather afraid I forced my way up here. The girl said you were busy but——'

Peter Blane waved away his protestations. 'She's new to the job.' He got out a big-bowled pipe and began to fill it. 'The hotel business isn't exactly a snip, Mr. Bentley. We get long queer hours and long queer problems. When I come up here, I like to be able to relax for an hour or so. I like to feel there are going to be no interruptions. Sometimes I work—sometimes I don't. Sometimes I entertain a friend.' There was a little note of amusement in his voice and Mark Bentley felt suddenly cold.

'You haven't entertained my daughter here, Blane?'

Peter Blane was watching him coolly. 'So that's what you came about?'

'I'd like an answer,' Mark said quietly.

Blane sighed. 'And you shall have one. I've entertained your daughter here on several occasions and neither she nor I thought anything about it. You're not upset at that fact, Mr. Bentley?'

'I'm not,' Mark said. 'I know Jane pretty well. Too well to worry about her.'

'Then what is the reason for this little visit?'

'I'm not upset,' Mark said again. 'But her mother is.'

Blane puffed thoughtfully for a second or two. 'That's different.'

'I'm glad you realize it,' Mark said. 'You know what mothers are, Blane.'

Peter Blane chuckled. 'Not me. What are they?'

'Well, they don't think the same way as we do. They get a lot of damned queer ideas in their heads.'

'Such as what?'

Mark scowled. 'Damn it all, Blane, you don't make things particularly easy for me.'

'Is there any reason why I should, Mr. Bentley? All I can say is that if I do understand you, you've got some damned queer ideas in your own head. Ideas you'd better get rid of as soon as you can.'

'But they aren't my ideas,' Mark said. 'Haven't I told you that already, Blane? They're my wife's ideas.'

'That goes for her too, then,' Blane said calmly. 'I hate to seem churlish, Mr. Bentley—especially when I'm talking to a gentleman like yourself—and about a lady so charming as your wife is—but I'm afraid you don't leave me much choice.'

Mark Bentley sat back gloomily. 'Well, like it or not— my wife doesn't like to think Jane is spending so much of her time here with you.'

Amusement filled Blane's eyes. 'I can see your point of view, but seeing it, I don't think much of it. Have you told Miss Jane about this?'

'Good Lord no!' Mark was alarmed. 'You can't talk

14

like that to Jane. She says and does the most outrageous sort of things. I'll be quite frank with you, Blane. My wife's been worried about Jane for a while now. She's too free and easy—too thoughtless. She's been coming over here for months now—and people are beginning to talk about it. You don't want that, do you?'

Blane shook his head. 'Indeed I don't. Bad for business.'

Mark felt a momentary flicker of anger. He said shortly: 'All right, Blane. That's your angle. Bad for business. Mine is, it's bad for Jane. I've come over and put the matter to you as one gentleman to another. I'm expecting you to do something about it such as telling Jane not to come back.'

'You've tried that?'

Mark shook his head. 'Not me. I'm a lazy sort of devil. The line of least resistance has always been the line I've made for first. This time it's going to be a bit different. I'd ask you to remember it.'

Blane got up and went over to the decanter. 'Another drink?'

'No, thank you.' Mark rose, himself. In the moving, changing light Blane's features shifted almost grotesquely. Mark stared at him uneasily for a moment, more than half aware he had done but little to improve an awkward situation. 'Well, I'd better go. I'm sorry to have had to speak like this—but these sort of things happen, don't they? And when they do—well, you can't beat a little bit of plain speaking. After all, we're both gentlemen and——'

Blane chuckled. 'I shouldn't rely on it too much, Mr. Bentley. Still, I can see your point of view. Tell you what I'll do. I can't tell the girl to stop coming over. She likes the Knight Templar. She likes me—she likes being around. But I'll tell her you've called. I'll put it up to her. How's that?'

Mark stood still. 'You don't mean that?'

15

'What else can I do? I could certainly tell her not to come back, but that wouldn't work out. If you've got any ready-made solution I'll be glad to hear it.' He ushered his caller along the dimly lit corridor. 'Be careful of the stairway, Mr. Bentley. It's rather awkard.'

They negotiated it together and made their way to the rear of the house. Mark Bentley halted with one hand on the door. 'I've got the car out here. And I'd be obliged if you could do something to help. My wife's going through a bad patch just now and I don't want her upset. I do what I can to please her.'

'And rightly so,' Mr. Blane said jovially. 'I'm all for every man doing his best to please his wife. If everybody believed in your sentiments, Mr. Bentley, sir, we'd have a much happier world.' He held the door open wide. 'Look at that, would you now?'

In the pale shaft of light from the open doorway, sleet slanted down on the muddy surface of the court-yard. Mark pulled on his heavy driving-gloves. 'Well, that's that. Good night, Blane.'

'Good night, sir,' Peter Blane said pleasantly. He watched Bentley get into the car, start up the engine and pull out, then, raising his hand in salute, he closed the door.

Mark Bentley saw him withdraw as he swung out into the roadway. He waved one hand in farewell and drove off into the night, and as he went he was vaguely conscious of the fact that matters had scarcely turned out as he had wished. He drove disconsolately back to the Close, put the car into the garage then went inside.

It was almost six o'clock. At this hour Faith would be resting. He tiptoed along as far as the bedroom, listened at the door. Her breathing was deep and regular and from experience he knew that she would sleep till her maid wakened her at seven o'clock, to dress for dinner. Very quietly he made his way to the study. He sat down here, his pale blue eyes slow and pensive, then, leaning

16

forward he touched a bell on the underside of his desk. A housemaid appeared a moment later. She said, 'You rang, sir?'

Mark Bentley nodded. 'I did. Send up Clancy.'

3

CLANCY appeared almost at once. He was a small, slope-shouldered man with pale, weary eyes and an expression of unmitigated sadness. He wore a suit of levitical black and carried under his arm a dust-covered bottle of port, and Mark eyed him severely. 'What the devil is this, Clancy?'

Clancy laid the bottle on the table. 'Port, sir. I was in the cellar when I heard Ella calling for me. I'm about run off my feet these days. If it ain't one thing it's another. Did you want something?'

'I did,' Mark said. 'And I still do. First of all, take that filthy bottle off the table and pay attention. Where were you at four o'clock this afternoon?'

Clancy looked surprised. 'What's it matter, Mr. Bentley?'

'At four o'clock,' Mark said stonily, and waited.

Clancy considered. 'In the gun-room, I think. Or maybe I was in the billiard-room doin' a bit of dusting.'

'Or in your bedroom,' Mark said nastily, 'doing a bit of sleeping?'

Clancy made vast protestations of his innocence. 'As I live an' die, Mr. B, I must have been about the house, workin' an' slavin'. You got no idea of the jobs that's to be done. There's dusting—an' sticks an' coals—there's beer cases to handle an' dustin'—an' port to decant an' curtains to draw, vegetables to be brought in an'——'

'Dusting?' said Mark.

'That's right. Jobs, jobs, jobs. Sometimes I wonder how I keep up with it all at my age. I ain't so young as I was at one time.'

'Who is?' Mark eyed him with hostility. Clancy had been in his employ for close on twenty years now, was an inveterate grumbler, and completely loyal. He said slowly, 'Did you hear the telephone ring at four o'clock?'

'Did I hear the telephone ring?' The little man was cut to the quick. 'Imagine you askin' me that, sir! Did I hear the telephone ring? Is there anythin' that ever happens around his house I don't 'ear?'

'Well, did you?'

Clancy coughed. 'No. It so 'appened there was a little job to be done an'——'

Mark sighed. 'I thought not. Well, I did. I answered it in the study. That was at four o'clock. When I came out of the study there was someone in the corridor. If it wasn't you, I'd like to find out who it was.'

Clancy looked puzzled. 'At four o'clock! It wouldn't be cook, or Ella, or Connie, because they was in the servants' 'all as I 'appen to know. It wouldn't be Soper or Cass.'

'I don't want to know who it wouldn't be,' Mark explained. 'I want to know who it was. I'm leaving the job of finding out in your capable hands. I'll expect an answer. And now we'll turn to something else. I've got to go up to town at once.'

'At once? What's the idea? It'll soon be dinner. What's cook goin' to say about that? What's Mrs. B goin' to say?'

'You can tell me when I get back,' Bentley said pleasantly. 'In the meantime, let's have some action. You can pop down to the garage and get out the Humber. Take it down to the East Lodge gate and leave it there.

18

You can have the gates unlocked for me and close them when I'm gone. I'll be late. Make my excuses to Mrs. Bentley. That's all.'

Clancy turned on him the look of a wounded fawn. 'I've to do all that?'

'All of it—and at once,' Mark said firmly.

'I'll have to walk back from the East Lodge,' Clancy said indignantly. 'Me. 'Alf a mile, as near as you like an' it's raining cats and dogs. Did you forget that?'

'Take an oilskin,' Mark said. 'Now get out. I've got jobs of my own to do.'

The little man went out, grumbling, and when he had gone, Mark went over to the telephone. When he heard the voice of the operator, he said: 'This is Marchgate Priory 103. I want to put through a London call.'

Mark gave him the number, then came the voice of the operator. 'You're through now, sir.'

Mark said: 'Hullo, Hudson? This is Mark Bentley. I'm coming up to the City tonight to see you.'

Hudson said cautiously, 'At the office?'

'At the office. Are you busy just now?'

'Fairly. But if your job is important, I can shelve it for a little. When do you expect to be here?'

Mark thought it over. 'I've got another call to make first. Suppose we say ten o'clock at Bailiff's Court? I won't keep you waiting very much later than ten.'

'Ten o'clock,' Hudson said. 'I'll be there, sir.'

'Good.' Bentley hung up. For a moment or so he sat still, then made his way to the cloakroom, picking up a hat and a long, fleece-lined trench coat. He buttoned the coat high round his neck, pulled the hat low over his forehead then went out. He walked briskly down the avenue which led to the East Lodge, moving in the shelter of the trees. The red rear-light of the Humber blinked ahead of him in the darkness, and when he arrived at it, Clancy slid out from behind the wheel still protesting.

19

'Such a caper on a night like this. You'll get your death. So will I.'

Mark hitched up his coat and got inside. 'Stop complaining. You're the luckiest man I know, Clancy. A good job, comfort, and all the beer you want to drink.' He touched the starter, sat for a moment listening to the engine. 'Skip it, Clancy. And don't forget to leave the side door open for me—and to make my apologies to Mrs. Bentley.' He eased his foot up on the clutch and the big car edged away. He swung out into the main road, then turned towards Marchgate Priory and in a few moments the village lay below him. For an hour and more he drove at breakneck speed. Reading, Maidenhead and Slough fell away into the darkness and it was not until the streets widened and the traffic thickened that he reduced his speed, with one eye on the dashboard clock.

He was running well within his time, but there was the call he had mentioned to Hudson, and it was important that it should be made. He made his way to Chelsea, drove past the front of Chelsea Barracks then found his way to Marley Lane. No. 24 was a tall red-brick house in a block of six tall, red-bricked houses, and in front of this he drew up. He got out, locked the car and went up the four steps which led to the front door. On the second floor he went along to the end door. There was a white card inserted in a little metal holder, and on this was typed:

MRS. EVE BOLTON

For a second or so he stood there, then, very gently, he touched the bell. It rang quite close at hand, and before the peal had died away the inside light was switched on, the door opened and Mark Bentley took off his hat with an exaggerated politeness. 'Hullo, Eve. Big surprise, eh?'

She stood there looking at him. Eve Bolton was tall,

20

fair, and her features were well moulded, but over the years her figure had thickened, so that her shoulders were wide and fleshy, her face heavy with fat. For a moment or so she watched him, then Mark became aware of the odour of gin, superimposed on something sweet and cloying. 'Been at the bottle again, Eve?'

She stood back to let him come in. Mark walked past her and into the main apartment of the flat. It was a large room, well carpeted and furnished with a heavy cumbersome suite in uncut moquette of a peculiarly vivid rose colour. There was a profusion of cheap ornaments, figurines, chromium ash-trays, and mirrors under a film of dust. There was a bleary-eyed Pekinese on the sofa and a malevolent Siamese cat sat on the rug in front of the fire. He watched her come towards him and put a decanter on the table.

'Have a drink, Mark?'

Mark Bentley shook his head. 'Gin? Not on your life. That stuff's poison. Anyway, sit down. I want to talk to you.'

She poured out a drink for herself. 'Go on, Mark—but don't lecture. I'm in no mood for it. I wish you'd sit down and be sociable. I can remember when you quite liked to have a drink with me.'

'Skip it,' he said calmly. 'Don't start to argue, Eve. You're half soused or I don't suppose you'd trouble. You're on to quite a good thing and when you're sober you know it. Get sober again.'

She watched him, blinking a little. 'Good, did you say?'

'I did.' Mark was quietly contemptuous. 'Have you any doubts about it?'

Something in his voice stung her to fury. 'Why shouldn't I have doubts? What sort of life is this for a girl anyway?'

'Shut up, Eve.' His voice was quiet. 'You're wasting my time. Worse than that, you're wasting my money.

21

We can't have that, can we? All this tawdry finery—
filthy little dogs and silly cats.' He prodded the Siamese
with his toe. 'How much did that beauty cost?'

She thought. 'Ten pounds, but——'

'That's what I mean. Cats you can get a hundred for
sixpence. Nicer looking creatures than this horror, too.
You're well off, Eve. You live comfortably—and you
do it at my expense. Sometimes I wonder if it's all worth
while. Eve, when I get around to thinking like that—
you'd better watch your step.'

'What do you mean?'

Mark smiled benevolently. 'I mean I've had about
enough. I always pay well for services rendered, but it's
a long time since you rendered any. One of these days
I'm going to get fed up. When I do'—he snapped his
fingers—'there's an end to all this. Just like that. You
won't like it much.'

She stared up at him, white-faced. 'You wouldn't
dare! If you did—you'd be sorry for it.' There was rage
in her eyes but it burned itself out in the calmer stare of
his own. For a moment or so he looked down at her,
then:

'I've warned you before. Watch your step. Watch your
company. I've had a report about you I don't like. This
is your last warning, Eve. Don't say you've never had it.'
There was an odd finality in his voice. She pushed away
her empty glass. For once she was humble as she looked
up at him.

'I'm sorry, Mark. I didn't mean to make you angry.'

'You didn't care whether you did or not.' He began to
walk towards the door.

She followed him. 'Mark, don't go away in a mood
like this. If you do it leaves me upset and that's when I
drink.' She got between him and the door. 'Sit down
for a moment or so and talk it over. What sort of a life
have I here—in this dump?' She looked around her.

Mark said: 'Does it need to be like this? All these cats

and things? All this blowsiness? The answer to that one is it never was any better at any time.' He pushed past her to the door. 'I'm going now, Eve. Think it over.' He opened the door and went into the hall, closed it behind him, then went down to the car. There had been a time when she had been a necessity to him. Now she was an encumbrance who might well prove to be a menace.

4

IT WAS almost ten minutes past the hour when the big car drew up in front of No. 11 Bailiff's Court and Mark Bentley climbed out. Bailiff's Court was old, dilapidated and out of date, but there was atmosphere about it and Mark Bentley, who was unaccountably sensitive to atmosphere, never came here but he was aware of an aura of the past. He made his way to the second floor, halting in front of a door. On it in faded black letters was printed:

GARNETT AND HUDSON
Private Investigators

He knocked heavily on the panel and immediately heard the sound of someone approaching. The door opened and Hudson looked at him. 'Good evening, Mr. Bentley. Come through this way.' He closed the door, turned the key in the lock, then led the way through to a small room which opened off the outer office. There were two well-worn armchairs and Lew Hudson indicated one of these. 'Sit down, Mr. Bentley.'

Mark sat down, fumbling for a cigarette. Lew Hudson took the chair across from him. He was a lean, wiry man who had spent some ten years in the Metropolitan Police. When he had settled down, he said, 'Well, Mr. Bentley, what's it all about?'

Mark leaned back. 'I want you to do a little bit of checking up for me.'

'On whom?'

'I don't know yet. That's what you've got to find out.'

'Suppose you tell me about it, Mr. Bentley.'

Mark smiled without humour. 'I'll give you all I can. You'll have to find out the rest for yourself. In the past week or two, someone's been ringing up at my house. All I can tell you is that it's a man.' He spoke for a matter of five minutes and Hudson listened, interested. At the end of that time he took the pipe from his mouth.

'And how often then would you say you've had a call from this fellow?'

'Four times,' Mark said. 'Always around four o'clock. He never varies very much.'

'And always the same voice?'

'Always.' Mark thought for a moment. 'Yes—definitely always.'

'It couldn't be anyone you've met?'

'It could be,' Mark said. He chuckled softly. 'I've got my own ideas, Hudson—but I could be wrong about it. Anyway, I want you to take it in hand. I want you to find out who's responsible for it. That's all.'

'And what happens when I find out?'

'You can leave that to me,' Mark said. 'It may be a joke. I don't know about that. If it is—I can't think why. But I'm going to find out.'

There was a flat little silence. Hudson smoked pensively. 'Whoever he is—he has to be local. It's never been a trunk call. That should make it easy. How many telephone kiosks are there in the neighbourhood?'

24

'Two. One in the village itself, one at the cross-roads about a mile out.'

'It shouldn't take long,' Hudson said. 'I'll have a word with the operator. Who runs the village post office?'

'There is none,' Mark said. 'The post office is at Ferndale which is about three miles away.' He produced his wallet and took out a little pad of notes. 'How much?'

Hudson's eyes flickered. 'We'll say fifty for expenses, Mr. Bentley. I won't count my time just now. These jobs have a habit of stretching out. I don't want this one to do that. I've got a lot on my mind these days.'

'Who hasn't?' Mark said. He counted out ten crisp, white notes. 'There you go. And I want this settled.'

Lew Hudson gathered in the notes. 'It can be done all right. If not, I'll be very surprised. You got my report on Mrs. Bolton?'

'I got it,' Mark said grimly. 'I called on her tonight.'

'I wondered if you would,' Hudson said. 'She's been seeing a lot of this fellow Varney. I don't say that it isn't all entirely harmless. It may be, but the neighbours don't think so.'

'You've been talking to the neighbours?'

'Off and on. After all they're the only people who can tell you anything at all.'

'What does Varney look like?'

Lew Hudson considered. 'Maybe about fifty-five and rather grey. He dresses well. Five feet ten or so; thick-set and with a bit of a limp.'

Mark turned the information over in his mind. 'I can't think of anyone who looks like that. You can continue to keep an eye on her.'

'I'm going to have to turn it over to Colling, if I've to handle this other thing.'

Mark looked thoughtful. 'He's quite reliable, is he?'

'Quite. The old man doesn't come in much now. He's had his day of it.'

'Will he talk?'

25

There was a thin smile on Lew Hudson's dark features. 'Not Tom Colling. I can't think of a better man. I'll have a word with him tomorrow. Anyway, he knows about the job.'

'Make it tonight,' Mark said.

Lew Hudson looked surprised. 'Does it have to be that way?'

Mark nodded. 'I want you to start on this job as soon as possible. That means tomorrow. You'll come to Marchgate Priory in the morning. There's a hotel there. The Hotel Knight Templar. It's run by a fellow called Blane. So far as I know you'll be comfortable.'

Lew Hudson knocked out his pipe. 'I'll attend to it, sir. Tomorrow.'

Mark looked at him a little curiously. 'Are you a married man?'

Hudson shook his head. 'Not me. Always had to work too hard to worry about women and when I was in the Force the hours were too uncertain. Maybe I'll get round to it some day.'

Mark rose. 'Well, you can get started on this job tomorrow. Colling can look after the other angle till you get back. You haven't located Varney yet?'

'I haven't,' Hudson said regretfully. 'I've only seen him twice and I couldn't be too near. Once he's seen me —I'm out of it.'

'That's true.' Mark Bentley moved over towards the door. He opened it, and passed out into the larger room beyond, and as he did so there was the sound of a door closing quietly ahead of him. He swung round. 'What was that?'

Lew Hudson had heard nothing at all. He brushed through, opened the office door and stepped out into the corridor. For a moment or so he stood there listening. 'Sounds like someone on the stairs,' Hudson said softly. 'Maybe I'm wrong. You come down at my back.'

Mark followed on silently but with less celerity. When

26

he reached the ground floor he saw the figure of the detective standing at the entranceway, peering up and down the short street, and he went forward to join him. 'Did you see anyone?'

Lew Hudson looked puzzled. 'I thought I did. There was someone on the street, but he was too far away to be seen.' He walked back towards the stairway, his eyes on the grey stone slabs of the floor. 'Come here, sir.'

Mark followed him back. Hudson was staring at one or two confused footprints on the floor. He said, 'Some of these are probably your own.'

'I came by car.'

'I know. But the pavement is still wet and muddy. You'd make some kind of mark. There are several here, but anybody could have made them. A policeman having a smoke—somebody sheltering from the rain. Maybe somebody going up to the flats above.'

'There are flats above?' Mark was surprised.

'Caretaker's,' Hudson said. 'He's a retired policeman and he's got a large family. Maybe it was one of them. I'll find out later.'

Mark patted his shoulder. 'Do so. And now you'd better get back upstairs, Hudson. Good night to you.'

Lew Hudson agreed. 'Good night, sir.' He waited until Bentley had got into the Humber, then, with a wave of his hand, he moved out of sight.

Mark watched him go, switched on and ran the motor for a moment or so. It was going to be late indeed before he could manage to return to Marchgate Priory. He drove on through the night, his eyes fixed steadily on the white ribbon of road which stretched out interminably before him, and in his heart there was a queer cold dread.

5

IT WAS almost nine o'clock next morning when Mark Bentley saw Faith, for at nine she sent for Mark, and he came up, penitent.

'Good morning, darling.' He leaned over to kiss her. 'Sit down, Mark.'

He sat down. 'You've had breakfast? Where's Jane?'

'Out, I suppose. I heard her moving around before it was clear.' Her voice altered. 'Where were you last night, Mark?'

'The City. Didn't Clancy tell you? The little devil! I'll wring his neck for him.'

He looked so suddenly furious that she smiled. 'Clancy told me all right—but you hadn't mentioned it.'

'Verrall rang up. There was rather an important decision that had to be made and I couldn't make it without advice from the man on the spot. I had to go through and see him. I was back here around one o'clock.'

She was satisfied with his story. Finance and its complications she neither understood nor wanted to understand and details of board meetings and all the mysteries of high commerce, she was prepared to relegate to oblivion. 'What a bore for you, Mark.' She leaned out to touch his hand. 'What about Blane? Did you see him yesterday?'

For the moment Peter Blane had slipped his memory. 'Blane? Oh yes, I saw him, Faith. In fact I had quite a talk with him.'

'And what did he say?'

Mark pondered. It was rather difficult to recollect just exactly what Blane had said. Now he temporized. 'It wasn't so much what he said as what I said.'

He told her with some little licence what he had said, and Faith listened unimpressed. When he had finished, she said, 'Did you really say all that, Mark?'

Mark coloured. 'Well, most of it. I told him we didn't want Jane to be going there any more.'

She sighed. 'Bringing up a daughter is such a responsibility, Mark, especially a daughter like Jane. If only she would listen to advice. I thought St. Elma's would have changed her, but it didn't. Not a bit of it.'

'Nothing will change her,' Mark said gloomily. 'Nothing unless it's marriage. If she'd only pay some attention to Johnny, but she looks down her nose at him, and I can't think why. Johnny's a nice chap. One of the best.'

Faith had a soft spot for Johnny Selwyn herself. 'So well off, too, isn't he, Mark?'

Even Mark was prepared to admit that Johnny Selwyn was comfortably off by the most exacting standards. 'He's got pots of money, but that doesn't seem to matter to Jane.'

'She's like Tommy,' Faith said in exasperation. 'Tommy never could understand money. That was what so upset me about him. Nobody could ever be less mercenary than I am, but all my life I've realized you have to have a certain amount of it. Tommy could never see that.' She frowned as she reflected on this remarkable and reprehensible trait of the late Tommy Osborne, then became instantly practical. 'I think we should ask Johnny down again.'

'She wasn't very nice to him last time, was she?'

'I'll have a talk with her.'

'I don't see that that will do any good. You can't get round Jane by talking to her, but it might not do any harm to have Johnny come for the week-end.'

'This is Friday,' Faith said firmly. 'Ring him up, Mark. Ring him up now.' She pointed to the telephone on the bedside table.

He thought it over, lifted the receiver and gave a number. 'Call me back when you get through, operator.'

He had not long to wait. A moment more and he heard the rather clipped voice of Johnny Selwyn. 'This is Mark Bentley, Johnny. We want you to come along for the week-end. Can you come tonight?'

'Like a shot, old boy.'

'Good. We'll expect you in time for dinner.' He spoke for a moment more then hung up. He looked round at Faith, smiling. 'That's that, Faith. He'll be company for you and Jane. Verrall's coming in the late afternoon. I may ask him to wait overnight.' Mark grinned. 'You've never liked Verrall, have you?'

Faith admitted it honestly. 'I think he's such a sinister-looking man. I don't know how anyone can ever trust him with large sums of money and things like that. He's got very shifty eyes. Besides he bets on horses and things. I'm positive he'll be up to all sorts of artfulness.'

Mark, who loved a flutter himself, was honestly amused. 'It doesn't seem a great deal of evidence on which to condemn a man,' he protested.

It was enough for Faith. 'I wish he wasn't your lawyer at all. I've always wished that. I'm going to get up at ten, Mark. There's such a lot to be done. I'll have to tell Clancy that we've got people coming. Goodness knows what he'll say.'

'I can guess,' Mark said. He rose now. 'I'll get along to the study, dear.' He walked to the door, then halted. 'And if you have an opportunity you might tell Jane that Johnny will be here tonight.'

Faith sighed. 'I'll tell her—for all the good it will do. I never met a girl with less romance in her. You'd think she'd be delighted to think that a handsome young man like Johnny Selwyn was so fond of her—but not Jane. She's much more interested in dogs, or fishing, or some dissolute old barman who lets her help in his filthy hotel.'

'It isn't exactly a filthy hotel,' Mark said. 'In fact, it's jolly nice.'

'Dyer says she heard that Jane was serving in the bar, one night.'

Mark Bentley laughed aloud. 'Jane was! Good Lord! She'll be wanting me to buy her a pub next.'

'It's nothing to be amused at.'

'I don't suppose it is,' he agreed soothingly. 'After all, few fathers want their daughters to become barmaids. And yet there's very little wrong with a good barmaid.'

She laughed suddenly. 'Well, we don't want Jane to be one. But you know what I'm afraid of. She's so outrageously headstrong and there's no saying what she'll do next. She'll probably turn round and marry someone quite ghastly like that grocer in Sevenoaks.'

'That wasn't very serious,' Mark said. 'And anyway he wasn't a grocer.'

'His father was—and he'd worked in the shop quite often. Then there was that medical student from Canada.'

'Young McLean?' He frowned at the recollection. 'That might have been a lot more serious. I think we got out of that one quite fortunately.'

Faith thought so herself. 'If it hadn't been for Dyer, we'd never have known about it. Dyer's got all her wits about her and it's just as well.' She thought of her thin-lipped maid. 'I'm going to ring for her now, Mark. You'd better go.'

'Of course. I'll see you later.' He went downstairs to the study, and had just sat down when Clancy came in, a feather duster tucked under one arm.

'It's yourself, Mr. B. I've been lookin' for you all mornin'.'

'Put that brush down,' Mark said, 'and come over here.'

'Taintabrush,' Clancy said, 'Safevverduster,' and for one second Mark Bentley thought he was speaking a foreign language.

Clancy looked at Mark wearily. 'Nothin' doin', Mr.

Bentley. I've been round 'em all. Cass, Soper—none of 'em was in the 'ouse at the time. It wasn't none of the inside staff, so it looks like you made a mistake.'

'I don't think I did.'

'Then who could it be?' Clancy looked a little perturbed. 'You got any ideas?'

'One or two,' Mark said. 'You keep your eyes open, Clancy, we don't want any trouble of any sort at this late day. It's a lot better to be safe than sorry. And it's a lot cheaper, too.'

The little man nodded. 'I know what you mean, sir.'

'Good.' Mark dismissed the subject with a nod. 'Now something else. Mr. Selwyn is coming for the week-end tonight. Mr. Verrall will be here, too. Verrall will stay overnight. I don't know just where Mrs. Bentley will want them put.'

'West wing,' Clancy said. 'West wing it 'as to be. I'll tell 'er that, Mr. B.' He went out leaving Mark Bentley to struggle alone with the intricacies of a correspondence which was rarely intriguing. At ten o'clock he halted to put through a call to London and a moment more a woman's voice said in his ear:

'This is Verrall, Merton and Trace.'

'This is Mark Bentley. Put me on to Mr. Verrall please.'

'Just a moment, sir.' There was a little humming sound then Verrall's voice.

'Hullo there. Mr. Bentley? This is Verrall speaking.'

Mark said: 'Come down tonight, Verrall. You'd better come prepared to stay the night. And, by the way, in case there are any questions asked, this was arranged yesterday. You understand?'

'Of course.' Mr. Verrall was particularly adept at understanding such instructions. 'I shall arrive sometime before seven o'clock. Give my regards to Mrs. Bentley.'

'I will,' Mark said. 'And we'll see you at seven.' He hung up, lit a cigarette then strolled over to the window.

32

For a moment or two he stood there, his keen blue eyes peering over pleasance and weald. To the right of him rose the high lands of Marchgate Close—the Quarry wood, the Knight's Ridge, and beneath it, grey and sullen in the November light, the leaden waters of Lady's Lake. There were seven thousand acres here. Seven thousand acres of good Berkshire land. Eleven farms, four villages, standing timber that was worth ten thousand pounds of anybody's money. There were other assets too numerous to mention. He wondered just exactly what it would be like to lose all this. Verrall had been nervous for some time now—but Verrall was a pessimist and always had been. The door opened suddenly and he swung round. For a moment he stared, then said with a certain weary resignation:

'Jane. Come in, my dear.'

She came in. The door closed.

6

JANE BENTLEY stood just inside it, looking at him. She was tall and slim. She wore her long fair hair hanging over her shoulders and she had the sort of look in her eyes that Mark Bentley had come to dread. They were grey eyes, laughing eyes, gay eyes, and defiant eyes. Mark, who had seen them in every mood, surveyed her warily. She came right across to where he was standing. She wore a tartan skirt and a bottle-green jumper. Then, after a moment she said, 'Hullo, Mark.'

Mark eyed her circumspectly. 'What's on your mind, Jane?'

She sat down on the desk and began to swing her legs. They were long, slim legs. Very much like Faith's own legs; only longer, just as Jane was taller. For a moment she sat like that, then, 'Mark, I'm in trouble.'

He was a little relieved. Jane in trouble was normality itself. 'What sort of trouble?'

'Pretty bad. Can you lend me five hundred pounds?'

Mark choked. 'Five hundred pounds? Can I lend you five hundred pounds? Of course I can't.'

'You could if you wanted to.'

'I don't want to. Anyway, I'd need to give it to you. You couldn't pay it back.'

Jane said: 'I don't suppose I could. That was really why I hoped I could get it from you, Mark. Just so that I needn't have to pay it back. Five hundred pounds would be a horrible millstone round my neck, wouldn't it? I'd just hate it.'

'Then you'll be glad you're not getting it,' Mark said with heavy humour. 'Well, it's nice to know it's all settled just so easily. All's well that ends well. What on earth do you want five hundred for?'

'I wanted to help a friend.'

'Who is the friend? It isn't Blane, is it?' He knew by the look in her eyes that his guess had been right. 'What the devil is the idea, Jane? Why should you want five hundred pounds to help him?'

'He's in difficulties,' she said calmly.

'How do you know? Did he ask you for the money?'

'No.' She laughed grimly. 'I can read, can't I? I wish you'd agree. You've got plenty of money.'

'Have I?' He smiled mirthlessly. 'It may come as a shock to you to know I haven't got just as much as I need for my own purposes.'

She looked at him in surprise. 'But we've got so much.'

'We've got it because we had it,' he said bluntly. 'If we lost a lot of what we've got just now we couldn't replace it.'

34

'I'm sorry, Mark. Forget that I asked you about it.'

She waved her hand then opened the door and had reached the hall when Mark recollected something. 'Just a moment, Jane. Your mother has been a bit upset recently because you've been spending so much time at the Knight Templar.'

Jane turned slowly. 'What's wrong with it?'

Mark scratched at his ear. 'Nothing much. I can't really explain her ideas to you—but anyway you're old enough to know what I mean.'

She said quietly: 'I like being at the Knight Templar, Mark. I like Peter Blane. I like the people I meet there. It's quite good fun helping out. I'm doing something when I'm there. Here I'm only wasting my time—waiting for something to happen. I don't want to spend my life like that. Do you think I should?'

He was irritated. This slim child had the knack of making him more uncomfortable than anyone he had ever met. 'I don't think we should go into that, Jane. You have to respect your mother's wishes. That's only fair.'

'I don't know that it is.'

'Good Lord!' Mark was a little scandalized. 'What's wrong with it?'

She surveyed him appraisingly. 'You're a bit old-fashioned, Mark!'

'Me? Me, old-fashioned? Don't be silly, Jane.'

She laughed gently. 'It's true. Not so old-fashioned as Mummy. I don't know why she should be like that. She must have had plenty of fun in her day. She was married when she was eighteen. I'll soon be twenty-two—and yet she worries.' She leaned over to pat his hand. 'Maybe it's her nature. But don't you worry, Mark. Promise.'

'I'll promise,' he said weakly.

'Good.' She swung round and walked briskly along the length of the hall. Mark could be very easily shocked.

She'd found that out a long time before and had made one or two highly interesting experiments. She went up to her room, threw off her coat and went through to where her mother sat reading in the morning-room. She came in almost jauntily. 'Hullo, Mummy. I've been down at the Quarry. Cass says there's a badger there by the old drain. He's going to dig him out.'

'Let him,' Faith said. She was city bred and had little interest in matters pertaining to drains or badgers. 'I hope you've got no other engagements for the week-end, Jane. We've got people coming. Mr. Verrall and Johnny Selwyn.'

Jane sat down on the arm of a chair. 'And I suppose Mark will be closeted all the week-end with old Verrall and you and I will be stuck with Johnny?'

Faith was shocked. 'Johnny Selwyn is one of the nicest young men I know. I don't know why you always snub him and talk about him so.'

Jane looked at her thoughtfully. 'Johnny isn't a young man. Not what I call young.'

'He can't be any more than thirty.'

The girl laughed a high note of scorn. 'Mummy, he's thirty-five if he's a day. He's so old his knees creak. And he will insist on being so damned rakish.'

'Don't swear,' Faith said firmly. 'Anyway, I think he's nice. Very nice—and very wealthy. I don't know why you can't encourage him a little more. He'd make a very good husband.'

'Not for me.'

'For anybody,' her mother said. 'You're twenty-two, Jane. When I was your age I'd been twice married.'

'I'm a later starter.'

The elder woman shook her head severely. 'You shouldn't joke about these kind of things. Your trouble, Jane, is that you won't ever take anything seriously. It worries me so.'

The door opened as she spoke. Dyer, her maid, said:

'Telephone, madame. It's the Lady Saltingham. She wants to speak to you.'

'Of course.' Faith went quickly from the room. Jane watched her go, then followed a little dejectedly along the hall.

Half past ten only. There would be the long interminable wait till one o'clock lunch; afterwards the dreary afternoon stretching on to late dinner. She wondered if they ever understood how boring it all was to her. She made her way outside, walked round the house to the outshed where she kept her bicycle. She carried it out, freewheeled down the long slope of the carriageway, and out through the East Gate, leading towards Marchgate Priory.

It was disconcerting that Johnny Selwyn was to be here for the week-end. She was under no illusions as to his precise feelings for her. Johnny was nice enough, and he was fond enough of her, but Johnny was dull. Apart from that, there was an excellent, even an interesting reason why she should avoid him as much as possible. She crossed the bridge swinging into the courtyard of the Knight Templar, and pulling up at the end of the garage, she leaned her bicycle against it then went inside. In the long back corridor she met the table-maid and the girl looked at her in some surprise. 'Good morning, miss. I didn't expect to see you so early as this.'

Jane laughed. 'I got bored. Where's Mr. Blane?'

'In the bar, Miss Jane. I'll tell him you're here.'

She made her way out to the lounge, where she stood for a moment or so looking around her, then made her way over to the windows.

Peter Blane came in briskly. 'Hullo, Jane. I was told you were here. I came along as soon as I could.' For a moment or so she saw the quizzical look in his eye and felt puzzled.

'What's wrong?'

Blane rubbed thoughtfully at his chin. 'I'm just

37

wondering. Have you had a session at this pleasant hour in the morning—or am I well off the beam?'

She looked at him reflectively. 'What made you think so?'

'I'm a mind-reader, my darling.' He laughed softly. 'And in addition to that I had mine yesterday afternoon. With Mark.'

'What did he have to say?'

He shrugged his broad shoulders. 'Just what you might expect. Mark's more than half a gentleman. Unfortunately he was batting on a fairly sticky wicket. In some ways he's got quite a nice mind.'

The girl laughed. 'I hope you weren't too sore on him?'

'I couldn't have been nicer,' he said evenly. 'He wanted me to discourage you from coming down here so much. Your mother doesn't like it.'

She was silent for a second or two. 'But you didn't agree?'

'No, I didn't agree—but I think we'll have to be a bit more careful. What do you think?'

She sobbed. 'It's all so difficult, isn't it?''

He took her in his arms and kissed her. 'I'm afraid it is. All we can do is be careful.' He let her go, then walked over to the door. 'We'll go upstairs. I want to talk to you.'

She went out in front of him, then the door closed. For a moment or so there was silence, then someone moved in the large, high-backed chair which stood facing the fire. Very cautiously Lew Hudson came to his feet and made his way over to the door. There was no sound at all and he slipped out. He made his way out to the old stone bridge which spanned the stream, sat down on the parapet of it and produced his large-bowled pipe. There was another man here—an older man who was obviously an inhabitant and for a moment or two, Mr. Hudson engaged him in perfunctory conversation. For half an hour they smoked and talked and at the end of that time, a girl came from the rear of the Knight Templar, wheeling a bicycle. Lew Hudson watched her without interest. 'Who's the young lady?'

His companion peered over the top of his spectacles. 'The young lady on the bike, sir? That's Miss Bentley from the Close.'

'Well, well,' said Mr. Hudson. Honestly surprised, he withdrew for lunch.

7

CLANCY, on a mission through the house, found Mark Bentley in the gun-room inspecting a gun he had recently purchased, and announced his presence. 'I been lookin' for you every place, Mr. B. You gives a man more work than enough that's all I got to say. Upstairs and down-stairs, I've been everywhere.'

Mark squinted at him along the barrel and made a suggestive little clicking sound with his tongue. 'Drop dead, Clancy!'

Clancy yelped. 'Whassat, Mr. Bentley? Put it down. You shouldn't ought to fool around with guns, pointing them at people. Put it down.'

Mark laid it back on the rack. 'What's the trouble?'

'Telephone,' the little man said. 'You all but put it out of my mind with your capers.'

Mark Bentley swung round. 'Telephone? Who is it?'

Clancy could give him no satisfaction at all. 'I asks 'im for 'is name but you might as well 'ave spoke to the wall. "Never mind that," 'e says. "You get Mr. Bentley for me. It's important," says 'e. Just like that 'e says it, so I've been lookin' for you 'igh an' low, in and out, ever since.'

Mark made his way wrathfully to the study and lifted the receiver. 'Hullo! Hullo? Is there anyone there? This is Mark Bentley.'

Somebody sighed. 'I was beginning to wonder, Mr. Bentley. This is Lew Hudson. I'm at the hotel. The place is deserted just now. I got here at ten o'clock. On a job like this it doesn't do to put off time. I've pushed one or two inquiries and I've got a list of every telephone in the district. Somehow I don't think this will be a long job.' There was something in his voice that sounded like elation and Mark Bentley seized on it.

'You've got something, have you?'

'I've got something,' Hudson said dryly. 'I'd like to have a talk with you sometime soon. I don't want to say anything on a country line, I've had some experience of them.'

'You can't be too careful.' Mark pondered for a moment. 'I've got some people coming for dinner. I might manage away about seven. How would that do?'

'Seven o'clock will suit me,' Hudson said. 'I can slip out of the hotel without much trouble. Where do we meet?'

Mark considered. 'It had better be here—at the Close. I'm seeing Verrall tonight. I can leave him with some papers to worry over for a half hour or so. You've got your car so you can come to the East Lodge. You can't mistake it. The West Lodge is occupied and it will be lit up. Pass it and the East Lodge is less than half a mile farther on. The house is empty and the gates are locked. I'll have them open for you. We can meet in the Lodge. You've got that?'

Lew Hudson had. 'Seven o'clock at the East Lodge, sir. I won't keep you long, but this is a queer business and I've got to have your opinion on it.'

'We'll go into it then,' Mark said. 'Good-bye.' He

hung up, lit a cigarette and sat there drawing on it. There was a flicker of interest and more than interest at his heart. There was some satisfaction in knowing this enterprising operator was on the job; still more in the knowledge that he had so quickly made some sort of discovery. He finished his cigarette, then opened a drawer of his desk. He drew out two keys, tied together with a length of strong twine, dropped them into his pocket and went out and along the hall. He drew on a long trench coat, lifted a battered hat from a peg and made his way quickly to the back door.

Clancy was in the courtyard when he went out and the little man halted as he came towards him. 'You goin' out, sir?'

'I'm going out,' Mark said. 'Not very far, Clancy. If it makes you feel any better I'll tell you this much, that I'm going to do a job which I could quite easily palm off on you.'

'I got plenty,' Clancy said. 'The mistress wants flowers.'

Mark got on his way. Five or six minutes took him as far as the cottage which at one time had been occupied by the lodge-keeper. It was a small, square building with pseudo-gothic towers, hidden from the drive by the tall spruce trees which had encroached over the years. He halted when he reached the porch of the Lodge, stepped into the shelter of it for a moment or so.

It was all but dark now. He moved over, fitted the key into the lock and turned it, trying the gates as he did so. They swung open silently on heavy, well-oiled hinges. He pushed them shut again, then went back to the Lodge and tried the door key. The door opened, albeit protestingly. There were no lights, but from where he stood he was able to see a table and the outline of one or two chairs. He closed the door gently, then made his casual way back to the Close with the pleasing knowledge that his plans for the meeting had been made.

It was dark now, with the rain clouds hanging low

41

over the countryside and the wind murmuring in the trees. He made his way back to the house and was in the wide hallway when he met Jane coming from the study. She said, 'I've just been answering the 'phone, Mark.'

'Oh? Who was it?' There was no more than mild curiosity in his voice.

The girl looked a little puzzled. 'It was rather odd. Someone said, "Hullo, Mark," and when I answered, he said no more at all. He hung up right away.'

Mark looked surprised. 'You didn't recognize his voice?'

'No.' She sounded hesitant. 'I—I don't think so. You know what voices on the telephone are like.' She took his arm. 'Come and have tea. Clancy has just taken it in.'

They went along to the morning-room where a great fire burned in the open hearth. Faith Bentley was putting cream into the cups and Clancy was plugging in a standard lamp so that the light of it fell over her shoulder. For a moment or so, Mark surveyed this charming domestic scene in silence. There was a sudden gust of wind and raindrops rattled on the heavy glass of the window, so that Clancy looked round from his labours testily. ' 'Ark at it,' he said. 'Cats an' dogs. That's wot it is. Cats an' dogs.'

Mark chuckled. 'Be glad you're not out in it, Clancy. It won't be pleasant driving on a night like this. I hope Johnny gets down without any trouble. He ought to be here before long.'

Faith Bentley looked at the clock. 'Probably within the hour, Mark. Johnny is in the white bedroom and Mr. Verrall will be in the room above the study. Are you going to be very busy?'

'With Verrall?' He remembered his proposed meeting with Lew Hudson and set about preparing the ground for it at once. 'I'm afraid I am. I don't expect we'll be finished a great deal before midnight.'

42

Clancy sighed. 'Me, neither. I'll be lucky if I am.'

'I wasn't talking to you,' Mark said mildly. 'And if you've finished, Clancy, you can hop it. Go someplace else to loaf.'

The little man went out murmuring. Faith watched him go. 'Really, Mark, I wish you wouldn't talk to Clancy like that. You encourage him and I'm always trying to improve him.'

Mark chuckled. 'You won't improve Clancy. He is what he is and nothing will change him.'

Jane said: 'Clancy's all right, Mummy. You don't need to worry about him. How long have you known him, Mark?'

'Twenty years or so.'

She digested this item of information. 'It's a long time. Before you knew Mummy?'

'Yes, a year or two before.'

'Then that makes it more than twenty years.'

'Does it?' He was a little amused. 'Perhaps you're right, Jane. I'm getting old, I suppose.'

Jane lifted her teacup. 'Where did you meet Clancy?'

For a second there was an odd little light in Mark Bentley's eyes. 'In London,' he said. 'Stop asking questions, Jane, and have another muffin.' He reached down the silver dish which held them and as he did so they heard the sound of a car pulling up the driveway towards the house.

Faith looked up. 'That's someone arriving. You'd better go down and find out who it is, Mark. If it's Johnny, bring him up here.'

He lifted his cup and drained it and had gone as far as the door when it opened. Clancy poked his head in uneasily. 'This is the start of 'em,' he said. 'Just arrived. Got as much baggage as if he was here for the rest of the month. I bet he's waitin' for me to go down an' carry it up. It's Mr. Selwyn.'

8

JOHNNY SELWYN came up a moment later. He was a tall young man, rather broad of shoulder and with tanned brown features which were in themselves pleasingly ugly. He came in now, grinning, an imposing parcel under his arm. He laid it on a convenient table then shook hands all round.

'Hullo, Faith. I've brought you some books.'

Faith said: 'You're a darling, Johnny. A new book is always such a joy.'

He looked over at Jane. 'I didn't bring you anything, Jane.'

'I should jolly well think not,' Jane said. 'I can buy my own books, can't I?'

Johnny grinned. 'I'll bet you can. Temper, temper! Hullo, Mark.'

Mark had been inspecting the parcel. He had stripped the wrapping from one of the novels and was examining the jacket without enthusiasm. 'What made you buy this kind of thing, Selwyn? I read a book by this character once before. It made me slightly sick. Got a mind like a cesspool. Dirty words, dirty ideas, dirty people.' He dropped it on the table. 'Don't you read it, Jane.'

She looked honestly interested. 'If it's like that, Mark, I might have a look at it.'

'Don't be silly,' Faith Bentley said. 'We're just having tea. Do you want tea, Johnny? Come over and sit down beside me.'

'He wants a drink,' Mark said with conviction. 'That's what he wants. Me, too.' He made his way out to the corridor then along to the study. He put a decanter and glasses on a try then went back. Johnny Selwyn was standing with his back to the fire, listening to Faith. His hair was fair and wavy and one lock of it hung like a tendril over his forehead. Mark began to pour out.

'Here you are, Johnny. Better for you than tea.'

Johnny accepted it gratefully. 'I've been thinking about this one for the last hour or so.' He dug out a worn old pipe and began to fill it. Mind if I smoke, Faith?'

'Not at all. I rather like a pipe,' Faith said. 'Why don't you smoke a pipe, Mark?'

Mark poured out a drink for himself. 'No use. I've tried it. Anyway pipes are a racket now. You can't look at an advertisement without seeing some character with a pipe in his mouth. Pipes are the hallmark of solidity and respectability. The advertisements prove it. I'm neither solid nor respectable.'

'You would look like you were, if you smoked a pipe,' she said. 'What do you think, Johnny?'

Selwyn chuckled. 'I'm easy. Don't drag me into it.'

Faith rose. 'Ring for Clancy to clear the things away, Jane. Mark, I want you to come along with me for a little. There's something I want to say to you. You don't mind if we leave you for a moment, Johnny. Jane can keep you company. Come along, Mark.'

Johnny watched them go out. When they had left the room, he looked over to Jane. 'Tact,' he said simply. 'The old people sheer off and leave the young birds together.'

She looked at him coldly. 'Why should they?'

'Can't you guess? Don't let it make you feel uncomfortable. I've got used to it myself. People are always doing it to me.'

'Why?' She looked at him calmly.

Johnny shrugged. 'I suppose I'm very attractive.' There was a little twinkle in his eyes. 'In fact I've heard it said that I am. Quite an enriching experience, too, I can tell you.'

'You're not very attractive to me,' Jane said frankly. 'You're too old.'

45

Johnny was a little wroth. 'My dear child, what does a year or two matter? Age is a relative term. I can think of quite a lot of girls I know who make a play for me.'

She was interested, possibly even sceptical. 'Where?'

'We won't go into that, old girl. You know how it is. Painful business altogether. I feel guilty. May even have been my fault, though God knows I was never serious about it. I suppose I've always been a bit of a charmer— but there you are. Fellows like me don't really realize the effect we have on the susceptible female heart.'

'I've never heard you talk like that before.'

'That,' said Johnny, 'is because, for the first time, you've seen me as I really am. Bold, handsome, dashing. The scales have dropped from your eyes, as it were.'

The door opened as he spoke. Clancy poked his head round it. 'They tells me the trays has to go down,' he said. 'It's a great life, Mr. Selwyn. Work, work, work— "In povery, 'unger an' dirt," as the good books says. 'Ow is things in London these days?'

'As usual.' Johnny knocked out his pipe. 'You don't get up to town much now, Clancy?'

The little man sniffed. 'It ain't easy. Sometimes I wish Mr. B would go up to town for a change. You misses a lot bein' in the country. No shows—no culture. I could do with a night at the old Windmill meself. Well, I suppose you can't 'ave everything.'

'Next time you come up to London let me know and we'll have a night at the Windmill together. On your way, Clancy. I'm going along to my room to unpack.' He went out, whistling softly. Clancy watched him to the door, winked at the girl.

'That's that. A fine feller, Mr. Selwyn. 'Im and me always got along fine.' He went out, closing the door behind him with his foot.

Jane watched him go. For Clancy she had a vague affection. The little man had been a member of the household for the whole of her lifetime and there had been occasions when he had been both companion and accomplice. Faith, herself, had never become used to him, but she did tolerate him with an air of weary acceptance. Mark came back into the room as she sat there, looking around him curiously. 'Where's everyone, Jane?'

'Johnny's gone to unpack. He left just a moment ago.' He stood by the door looking down at her. For a second or so he was silent, then, 'You don't like Johnny very much, do you?'

She wrinkled up her nose. 'Do I have to, Mark?'

He walked over towards her, his face was suddenly hard. 'I don't know that you have to. Your mother would be pleased.'

'It doesn't seem a very good reason to me.'

'Maybe not. I like to keep her pleased and when she makes up her mind about anything she usually gets her way.'

'I know, Mark. But it can't always be like that.'

'It always has been.'

She said slowly, 'Did you ever meet my father?'

He was a little taken aback. 'Tommy? No, I never met him.' He stared at her. 'You're a queer kid. You must take that side of your nature from Osborne. I'll swear you didn't get it from Faith.' He put both hands on her shoulders. 'Jane, you know we both want to do the best we can for you. Sometimes it's hard to tell what one should do for the best. Sometimes it's even impossible.' He dropped his hands suddenly. 'You haven't been at Blane's today?' So quickly did he change the conversation that she flushed.

'Yes. I—I—was. This morning.'

The hardness came back to his eyes. 'Why was that?'

'I wanted to,' she said rebelliously. 'I'm not going to stop, Mark. You've never forbidden it, Mark. I wouldn't like you to do that. I think if you knew him better and——'

'Knew whom? Blane?' Mark said quietly. 'Jane, are you fond of him?'

She held up her head defiantly. 'Yes, I'm very fond of him and——'

'Probably you are. You've been fond of people before. There was that Scotch doctor and——'

'Kenneth? Kenneth MacLean?'

'Was that his name?' He laughed shortly. 'Well, we won't say any more about it for the moment.' He stared at her moodily. 'You'd better go now, Jane.'

She went out, silently, puzzled, and upset by his attitude. When Mark was in this sort of mood, he was unpredictable. She made her way along towards her own room. Clancy was in the upper corridor when she went up, wrestling with a small walnut table. 'Mrs. B wants it in the dining-room,' he said. 'For coffee. We've got along fine without it for the three or four years we've been here. That's what I say. You would think I was a ruddy scene-shifter or a furniture-remover. Eight stone four, soakin' wet. That's me.'

Jane said, 'Do you want a hand with it, Clancy?'

The little man was shocked. 'Does I want a hand with it, miss? I should think not. I can manage fine. You see Mr. B?'

'Yes, I've seen him. He's in the morning-room.'

Clancy scowled. 'Passed me in the 'all with a face like thunder. What's got into him? That's what I'd like to know, eh?'

'Why don't you ask him, Clancy?'

Clancy lifted the coffee-table on to his shoulder. 'Not me, Miss Jane. Not when he's in that sort of mood.'

He walked slowly and stiffly along the hall, disappearing round a convenient corner. For a moment or so she hesitated, then made her way along towards her mother's room. She turned the handle of the door gently and looked in. The room was in darkness. Then, from the direction of the bed she heard a soft, choking sob.

'Mummy! What is it?'

There was a little creaking sound as Faith Bentley swung round towards her. 'Jane. What do you want here?'

'Why are you weeping?' the girl asked quietly.

'It's nothing—nothing at all. You must go now. Don't have Mark come back and find you here.'

She went a little closer. 'You've quarrelled with him, Mummy?'

Faith Bentley sobbed. 'Mark can be so difficult, Jane. Please go now. It would be so awkward and embarrassing for everyone if he came back.'

For a second or so Jane hesitated, then, very quietly, she left the room. If Mark could, upon occasions, be difficult, Faith Bentley could, without doubt, be singularly trying and she was in no mood to apportion responsibility for this particular incident. Miserably, she retired to the fortress of her own bedroom with the uncomfortable sensation that she had something particularly unpleasant to add to the sum of her own not inconsiderable worries.

9

IT WAS close on six o'clock when Mark Bentley made his way towards his bedroom, let himself into it and closed the door. Cautiously he crossed towards the door which led to the room his wife occupied. For a moment he stood there listening, then, gently, he turned the handle. 'Faith, are you there?'

She sobbed quietly in the darkness. 'I'm here.'

Mark pushed the door open more widely. He walked

across it towards her. She lay there, looking up at him. For a few moments he did not speak at all, then, 'I'm sorry, Faith.'

She gave a weary little sigh. It was but rarely that they differed, seldom indeed that they quarrelled, and when they had done so the pattern of reconciliation was invariably the same. Mark had always made the first approaches; Mark was always sorry for any opinion he had proffered, or even imputed. She did not speak, then in a little while he said, 'I said I was sorry, Faith.'

'I know, Mark. I heard you. But I don't know what you expect me to do about it. After all, it was you who lost your temper. You shouldn't have done that.'

'Maybe not.' There was a certain dryness in his voice.

She waited, then when he said no more: 'After all, Johnny is your friend. You would think you'd be glad if Jane married him. She's my daughter—and I'd be glad. Why can't you feel like that, too? You behave very strangely at times, Mark.'

'Perhaps I do, my dear, but I usually have reasons for my idiosyncrasies.'

She was prepared to admit the general truth of this, although still refusing to concede its validity in this particular case. 'I suppose you do, Mark. But I expect more sympathy from you than you've shown. After all, Jane is my only daughter. I'm ambitious for her. I want to see her safely married.'

Mark said bluntly, 'Safely married or happily married?'

Faith Bentley sat up in bed. 'Safely or happily married? What do you mean?'

He chuckled grimly. 'Think it over. Jane's no fool. Anyway she doesn't want to marry Johnny and there's no power in the land that can make her. Moreover—I don't think it would be such a good idea myself.'

She said: 'Mark, you're impossible. You've always made me think you were on my side.'

50

'I've changed my mind.'

'I can't understand you, Mark. I—I thought you'd come round to my way of thinking, but you haven't. You've got no proper appreciation of your responsibilities and——'

Mark Bentley stood up. 'Hell, Faith. Don't start all over again.'

She gasped. 'Don't you dare swear at me. Don't you dare lose your temper again.'

He stared down at her gloomily. 'All right—I'm sorry for that. You're not the only one who's upset, Faith. Don't you think we're both being rather foolish. My suggestion is we both forget it for a day or so. Let's get the week-end over then we can talk matters over. I want time to think about it all.'

'What do you want time to think about?' There was a thread of suspicion in her voice. 'I know you, Mark. You want to forget the whole thing and you imagine that if I say no more about it now, that that's over till the next time.'

He stood there staring down at her. 'Forget it, Faith. Let's have a drink. We'll kiss and make up. Later on I may have something to tell you.'

'What about?'

He hesitated. 'That can wait, too. Do you want a drink? Let me bring you one?'

She sighed. 'You can be such a darling, Mark. No, thank you. I don't want a drink. You go and have one with Johnny. You can't. There's a car arriving at the house. You'd better go down. That will be Verrall.'

'Damn Verrall!' Mark said. He leaned over to kiss her. 'All right, dear. I'll go down. See you later.' He went quietly from the room, closed the door then walked through his own bedroom to the hall. Clancy had gone out to the door. He heard the little man say:

'Come in, Mr. Verrall. His Nibs is upstairs. As usual I'm 'olding the fort. Is that all you've got with you? I'll pop up to your room with it. You go along to the mornin'-room. I'm glad you got 'ere safe an' sound. That's always sumfink, ain't it? Listen to the wind 'owl. An 'ell of a night to be on the road.'

Mark stepped out along the hall walking towards the wide stairway. Clancy he met on the first landing, a small week-end bag in his hand, a sneer of disparagement on his melancholy features. He held up the bag as Mark appeared. 'Take a look at that, me lord. That's no way for a gentleman to be travellin'.'

'Verrall?' Mark raised his eyebrows.

Clancy nodded. 'I sent the old perisher along to get a heat. Blue with the cold, he is.'

Mark prodded him in the chest. 'Clancy, you get more hopeless day by day. Sometimes I wonder how much longer I'll be able to put up with you.'

Verrall was in the morning-room when he went along. A tall, lean man and sallow of complexion, he stood in front of the cheerful fire. He swung round as the door opened. 'Good evening, Mark. I've just arrived.'

'I heard you,' Mark said. 'Faith is lying down and I was sitting with her.'

'Dear me!' The lawyer offered the conventional condolence. 'Nothing serious, I trust. I hope I haven't come at an awkward moment. If so——'

Mark shook his head. 'Not at all. She's just resting. Does it every day. Come and have a drink.' He led the way down the hall as far as the study. Here he held the door open for his guest. 'I'm glad you're here, Verrall. I've got a lot to talk about.' He looked at the older man moodily. 'You're not our only guest. Selwyn is here.' Mark handed across a glass. 'I'll see Johnny tomorrow.' He laughed harshly. 'I've got one or two things to say to him. How much are we down?'

Verrall coughed. 'I was just going to speak about that, Mark. In fact, I'm glad now you did ask me here tonight. I'm worried and——'

52

'You've got reason to be worried. How much?'

Verrall considered. 'Probably more than we expected. I'd say ten thousand.' He saw the younger man wince and added, 'That's at the outside, of course.'

'Over the last twenty years, Verrall, it comes to a lot, doesn't it? I make it close on seventy thousand.'

'Approximately,' Verrall said. He watched Mark with steady eyes. 'At the same time, Mark, I don't see what else you could have done about it.'

'There's always more than one way out of everything,' Mark said softly. 'Don't ever forget that, Verrall.'

The lawyer looked a little nervous. 'You may be right, Mark, but——'

Mark Bentley laughed suddenly. 'But I'm better off as I am? I've been doing a lot of thinking lately, Verrall. I've always been a pretty easy-going sort of fellow—but I've never been a complete fool.'

Verrall laid down his glass. 'We've had this sort of talk before, Mark. I don't like it. I'm involved, too. I wouldn't have done it for any other man. We've got to have it out now—once and for all. We've got to come to a decision.'

Mark Bentley smiled wryly. 'Later.' He looked at the clock. 'I'll have to leave you now for a few moments, Verrall. There's a little task I have to do. You can wait here if you like. Give me half an hour or so.'

'Of course, of course. I'll be glad to relax for a moment or so. Life is fairly hectic these days, Mark. The same old grind—the same old faces.'

'And the same old reward at the end of it,' Mark said softly. 'I know what you mean. You'll excuse me, Verrall. I'll see you later.' He went out, closing the door as he did so. It was a quarter to seven on the old clock in the hall as he went past it. He went through to the rear of the house and as he did so he heard the voices of the staff from the kitchen. He lifted a trench coat, drew on a hat and went

53

quietly along to the door, then stepped out into the night.

He walked smartly down towards the avenue, keeping close to the trees for shelter as he went. In a moment or two he had reached a bend on the driveway which took him out of sight of the Close itself. He walked on stolidly, aware that a crisis in his own affairs was impending, and conscious of the fact that its impact might have particularly unpleasing results.

He reached the gable of the Lodge, his eyes on the road. There was no glimmer of light, but it was possible that Hudson would park some distance away despite his instructions. He went out to the open road, stood for a moment then came back. As he did so he saw the dark figure standing on the porch and realized Hudson had been here before him. He moved towards him.

'We'll go inside,' Mark said. 'The door's unlocked.' He turned the handle. 'Walk straight ahead. There's a table and one or two chairs. You'll find some place to sit just ahead of you.' He fumbled his own way forward in the darkness, then sat down. 'Don't show a light. There's always the chance it might be seen. Now, Hudson, what have you got?'

There was a little click. A thin finger of light leaped across space and found his features. He blinked angrily in the glare of it. 'Damn you, Hudson, didn't I tell you not to show a light!'

There was a harsh little laugh. 'Sit still, Mark.' It was not the voice of Lew Hudson, but a harder and more hateful voice, and Mark Bentley did not move at all. In that moment a great deal of what had puzzled him was suddenly made crystal clear. He said thickly:

'It was you! I wondered——'

'That's right, Mark. You wondered. Now you know. Quite a good thing, too. It saves explaining.' The gun came up in his hand as he spoke.

Klop!

54

A little black hole appeared very suddenly between Mark Bentley's eyes. It seemed to grow just a shade bigger, then a trickle of blood began to glissade slowly down into one eye. Mark Bentley slid forward, then fell to his face. He lay very still, then there was the sound of a door opening and closing. The night was still again but for the hiss of the rain among the trees and the eerie song of the wind.

Something moved very gently in the shadows. The man who had been watching stepped out cautiously on to the grassy verge which led up to the door of the Lodge. Very quietly, very carefully, he made his way round to the stone porch, tried the door handle gently. It turned and he pushed the door open then stepped inside. He took an electric torch from his pocket, cupped his hand over the glass then pressed the switch. The light was thrown down to the floor, and moving forward he saw the huddled shape which lay there. For a second or two he stood, alarmed—startled into indecision, then he went down on his knees and made a brief examination. It was a moment or so before he rose, and when he did he made his way to the door, stepped outside, his ears alert and listening. Somewhere ahead of him someone was moving quickly along the thin gravel of the drive. For no more than a second did he hesitate, then a light shone on the road ahead of him and he heard the low beat of a car engine. He looked at his watch.

Seven o'clock! Lew Hudson arriving for his meeting with Mark Bentley.

'Poor Mark!' he said softly, and began to run.

10

IT WAS close on eight o'clock when Jane Bentley heard
the sound of a hurried footstep in the corridor, and a
moment later came a tap at the door. 'Come in. It's you,
Dyer. What do you want?'

Mrs. Dyer was a little out of breath. She was a stoutish
woman in her early fifties, had been Faith Bentley's
personal maid for several years now and was, by reports,
considerably in her confidence. 'Mrs. Bentley wants to
see you, Miss Jane. She's quite upset. You'd better hurry,
Miss Jane. The gong will soon be going and she wants
to see you before you go downstairs.'

'I'll go along at once.' The girl left the room and
made her way towards her mother's bedroom. She pushed
open the door and looked in. Faith Bentley was standing
by the communicating door which linked her room with
that of her husband. Jane closed the door behind her.
'What is it, Mummy?'

Her mother looked at her in exasperation. 'Jane, I wish
you'd stop calling me "Mummy". You're not a child
any longer and it makes me feel like a hag. You can call
me Faith. Everyone else does.'

The girl surveyed her calmly. 'I'm not going to call
you Faith. I don't like it. If you object to "Mummy",
I'll call you "Mother". Dyer said you wanted me. What
is it?'

For one moment it seemed that Faith Bentley might
flare up, then, surprisingly almost, she dropped her voice.
'All right, Jane. It's Mark. Have you seen him? He
hasn't come up to dress. He was here about an hour ago,
talking to me. Clancy's laid out his suit for him, but he
hasn't changed.' There was a note of irritation in her
voice. 'Dinner will be ready in a few moments now, and

he's nowhere to be found. Really, Mark can be in-furiating at times.'

'But isn't he with Johnny Selwyn?'

'He is not,' Faith said sharply. 'I sent Dyer down to find him almost half an hour ago. Clancy's looking for him, too. Really, it's most exasperating. I don't know whether to hold dinner or——'

Jane said: 'I don't see why you should. Not for long anyway. Go downstairs and have a drink with Johnny and I'll scout around for Mark.'

For a moment or so her mother thought the matter over. 'I suppose you're right, Jane. I'd better go down. Mr. Verrall is here, too. See if you can find Mark. He may have gone over to see Cass about something.'

Jane made her way to the back stairway and from there to the kitchen. There was no sign of Clancy there, but she met him in the corridor which led to the rear of the house, an exasperated man. He halted her indignantly. 'Ain't he turned up yet? It ain't like him to go off like that with the house full of people as it were.'

'Mummy thinks he may have gone over to see Cass.'

'Like enough that's just what 'e's done. I'll nip over an' give 'im a bit of my mind. Cass, too.' He made his way along to the back door and she heard his little exclamation of satisfaction. She followed him through to where he stood struggling into a voluminous Yarmouth. 'He's gone out right enough, miss. His coat an' hat's away. The old trench coat 'e always wears about the doors.' He opened the door. There was a little blast of cold air and a spatter of raindrops. Clancy stepped out into the night.

She made her way along to the study a little amused. Mark and her mother had had a difference of opinion. There had been a few words—and Mark had gone out to walk off his temper. It was not the first time she'd known him do that. She opened the study door and looked in. It was empty, but on the desk there was a silver tray, a

57

decanter and two used glasses, evidence in itself that Mark had been here with someone. She went back out of the room, and she was almost at the door of the morning-room when she heard the back door open and close.

She went back quickly towards it. Clancy appeared ahead of her a moment later, shaking the raindrops from his oilskins. She looked at him inquiringly. 'Did you see him, Clancy?'

'No, miss. I saw Cass. He's just come back to stoke up his fires for the night—but he hasn't seen Mr. Bentley at all. What do we do now, miss? Mrs. B is goin' to like this—not 'alf, she ain't. Cook's ragin' the dinner is goin' to spoil. I don't know where to look.'

'You'd better tell cook to serve dinner,' Jane said. 'Everybody's hungry and there isn't much use in up-setting things. He'll come wandering in halfway through it. You go and sound the gong. I'll find Mummy.' She went along to the morning-room, stood for a moment or so in thought, then opened the door. Faith Bentley and Johnny Selwyn sat in the big armchairs on opposite sides of the fire. Mr. Verrall was expounding some point of contention to which they both listened with polite boredom. Jane said: 'We're just going to have dinner. Cook is serving it now.' They heard the dull, hollow boom of the gong as she spoke, and Faith Bentley sighed.

'We'll go through, Johnny.' She led the way over to the door. Johnny followed Jane into the hall.

'Trust old Mark,' he said with some satisfaction. 'Never a dull moment. Would you care to take my arm, Jane?'

She said: 'Don't joke, Johnny. I'm wondering about Mark. It's not really like him. Mummy's quite angry.'

'I could see that.' Johnny Selwyn looked ahead of him to where Faith Bentley walked along with Mr. Verrall. 'I'd have asked her more about it, only that old goat wouldn't stop talking.'

They went into the dining-room, and took their places at the long table. Dinner was an unsatisfactory meal for all of them were conscious of the empty seat at the end of the table. Jane was glad indeed when the meal was over and they had returned to have coffee in the comfortable morning-room. Faith Bentley was more silent than was her wont; Mr. Verrall was clearly perplexed, and even the ebullient Johnny was a little more restrained than usual. It was not until they had finished their coffee that any further mention of Mark was made and then it was the lawyer who raised the subject.

'You don't think that anything—um—unpleasant might have happened to him, Mrs. Bentley? He may have had a fall or something like that. I remember a similar situation in which a client of mine who lived at Esher disappeared from his house one night and was lost for four days.'

Faith gave a little gasp. 'But Mark hasn't disappeared from his house. He's gone out for a walk and met somebody. Perhaps he's even gone down to the village and had a breakdown of some sort. Jane—send Clancy round to the garage to see if he's taken a car.'

Johnny Selwyn rose. 'That's a good idea. But if he hasn't, Faith, I think Verrall's right. I think we ought to do something.'

Faith Bentley put her hands to her head. 'But what can we do? We certainly don't want to make a fuss. Mark will be furiously angry if we do.'

'Then why,' Johnny said shrewdly, 'has he gone A.W.O.L.?' He crossed to the wall, touched the bell. 'Verrall's got the right idea there. He may have gone out for a walk and had a fall.'

'But it's raining,' Faith Bentley said. 'Simply pouring.'

'Mark liked walking in the rain,' Jane said quietly. 'We'd feel pretty foolish if we sat here all night and poor Mark was lying some place with a broken ankle or something like that.'

59

'My client at Esher had a fractured skull,' Mr. Verrall said darkly.

There was a little scream from Faith. 'I wish you'd stop frightening us, Mr. Verrall.'

The door opened and Clancy came in. 'There ain't no sign of anybody, ma'am,' he announced.

Mr. Verrall coughed. 'Quite so, Clancy. However, it has occurred to us that Mr. Bentley may have decided to make a sudden trip to the village. Will you be good enough to go along to the garage and see if a car is missing?'

Clancy shook his head. 'That's no good, Mr. Verrall. I've been.' He stuck up his hand counting off his fingers methodically. 'The 'Umber's there, the Land Rover's there, so's the Austin. That's 'em all. There's no cars missing. Neither yours or Mr. Selwyn's. Wherever he went he didn't go by car.'

There was a sudden uneasy silence. Mr. Verrall broke it. 'It looks to me as though something really ought to be done. I suggest, Mrs. Bentley, we take some sort of steps to see what we can do. It may——'

Jane said calmly. 'Mummy, we'll have to do something. Organize a search party or something.'

Johnny agreed briskly. 'That's so, Faith. We don't need to worry about the police for the moment, but we can get as many people together as possible and make a search. Clancy, you can dig out Soper and Cass. That makes five of us. Jane, you can come, too.'

Clancy withdrew speedily enough. Johnny looked round them all. 'The first thing we've got to do is to hold a little séance to see if we can find out where to look.'

Verrall said: 'I arrived at half past six. Mark came along a moment or two later and we went along to the study for a drink, and then Mark excused himself. He said he had some sort of task to attend to and he went out and left me there. That was a few minutes before seven o'clock. I finished my drink and looked at a copy

60

of *The Times* which was on the desk. I remember hearing seven o'clock chime while I was sitting there. I waited for about half an hour and when he didn't come back I went up to my room.'

No one spoke for a moment then Johnny said cautiously: 'It looks as though you've been the last person to see him, Verrall. We can check with Clancy and the staff. Suppose you and I go down to the kitchen, Faith, and have a word with the women.'

'I'll go,' Jane said. She went over to the door. 'Come on, Johnny.'

They returned in a moment or so. Verrall said anxiously, 'Have you found anything?'

'Only that Jenny heard someone go out by the back door,' Jane said. 'It was a few minutes before seven. It must have been Mark.'

There was a little silence, then the sound of footsteps in the hall. Clancy came in enveloped in a long wet Yarmouth. 'I've got Soper an' Cass,' he said. 'An' I've got Dave Pendleton, Soper's son-in-law that's come along to call on him. Are you ready, gents?'

'Give us a couple of minutes to get coats,' Selwyn said briskly.

Jane went out into the deserted hall and made her way upstairs to dress for the search, then made her way down to the main hall. Here they were waiting for her and Johnny had constituted himself commander of his force.

'We'd better pair off for this job, Clancy. You come with me. Soper and his friend can keep together. Verrall, you'll go with Cass.' He looked at Clancy. 'Where do we go from here, Clancy?'

Clancy said: 'If he went walking it ain't likely he'd leave the paths. Somebody 'as to go down the drive to the West Lodge an' out along the main road—maybe Cass and Mr. Verrall can do that. There's the road up past the ridge to the Mere. He often goes there. Soper can do that. It's a road he knows. You and me can go round the gardens, down to the pond an' through the orchard. When we get that done we've covered most of the likely places. You better come with us, Miss Jane. You can go through the green'ouses an' the garden. It ain't so wild there. 'Ark at the rain. Fair bucketin'.'

He opened the door and they passed out into the night. It was twenty minutes later that they came back to the gardens.

'Cold as charity,' Clancy said. 'An' soaked to the skin. Miss Jane, you ought to go back up to the 'ouse. Mr. Selwyn an' me'll walk the drive to the gates. What you want is a hot bath an' a nip of toddy.'

'I'll stay with you,' Jane said. 'Another quarter of an hour won't be so bad.'

Clancy spat feelingly. 'I don't know what Mark will say when he turns up. Well, we won't argue, miss. You take the right-'and side an' keep under the trees. Mr. Selwyn an' me'll do the drive an' the left.' He stepped out into the driveway and for close on ten minutes they walked, then the black outline of the East Lodge loomed up ahead of them in the darkness. A moment more and they had reached the gates; then Jane swung her torch across the roadway. For a second she stared in silence at the tyre marks inside the gates.

'Look, Clancy. There's been a car here.'

Clancy's own torch swung over the ground. 'What do you know, now? We should 'ave come 'ere first of all.'

Selwyn had crosssed towards them. 'Car tracks. Is that unusual?'

'These gates are always kept locked,' Jane said. 'Mark has the keys. It looks as though he's met someone here.'

Johnny tried the handle. It turned in his grip and as he leaned on it the massive iron gate swung open. 'It looks as though Mark has met someone and gone off with him. The gates haven't been locked because he expected to be back soon. Nobody living in here?'

'Not since we been here,' Clancy said. ''Tain't much of

an 'ouse. Mr. Bentley was talkin' about pullin' it down.'

Selwyn went across to the door. 'Locked,' Clancy said. 'Always kep' that way. Mr. Mark 'as the keys.'

Johnny tried the handle—pushing as he did so. The door yielded to him and he took one step forward. 'This time it's open, Clancy. Wait there. I'll have a look round. It seems queer it should be unlocked tonight.' He walked into the kitchen of the Lodge, fanning his torch around him.

Clancy was crowding the doorway. 'It's queer right enough, Mr. Selwyn. Never knew it to be unlocked before. Now how do you think——'

Johnny Selwyn cut the light of his torch suddenly. He swung round and collided with Clancy in the doorway. For one second there was a break in his voice. 'Stand still, Clancy.' He edged the little man forcibly out on to the porch. 'Get Jane out of here. Up to the house as soon as you can.'

Clancy sensed the urgency in his voice and stepped back on to the grass verge. 'What's wrong, Mr. Selwyn? Is 'e there?'

Johnny put one hand on his shoulder. 'He's there all right. You'd better get the police—and a doctor. So far as I can see Mark Bentley's dead—and my guess is he's been murdered.'

11

In the grey light of morning a large car left London, striking westward through Slough and Maidenhead as the first flush of dawn made a welcome appearance in the east, and Inspector Newall, but newly promoted, in the front seat of it, stretched his long legs wearily as the lights of Reading came up ahead.

'Not so much farther now. The road map says it's twelve to fourteen miles beyond Reading.'

Police Constable Russell was interested. 'Reading, did you say? I've seen that lot many a time. Perishin' hefty packet they are, too. Damn near chased Brentford off the field the last time I saw 'em play.' He relapsed into silence again for a moment, then: 'You know a feller who came from these parts, Know All? I'll tell you who. Sid Parker. Tall thin character with a beak on him like a parrot. Nosy Parker they calls him. They couldn't call him anything else.'

Newall smiled in the darkness. 'I remember him all right. So well I ought, Russell. It was me and old Mac-Pherson that took him, too. And while we're on the subject I'll bet you don't know who the original Nosy Parker was? That's a thing that not many people could tell you at all.'

Russell reflected. 'I've known a lot of 'em in my day. There was Nosy Parker that had a pub in Camberwell, and another one that was in the Guards with me when I was at Wellington Barracks. There was a Nosy Parker at Chingford when I was a young policeman. He was an inspector an' a proper bas——'

There was a rumbling sound from the rear of the car. Superintendent Flagg said: 'That's a fine way to talk about your superior officer, Russell. I could put you on a charge for that. You don't show a proper appreciation, Russell, of the honour it is to drive about with superintendents and inspectors like me and old Know All here. What was good enough for mere sergeants and inspectors won't do nowadays, my lad.'

'I begs your pardon, Mr. Flagg.' Russell apologized handsomely. 'I thought you was sleepin' or I wouldn't have taken the liberty.' He slackened off as the road

64

forked ahead of them. 'Which way is it, Know All? You've got the map.'

'Right,' Newall said. He fumbled in an inner pocket and produced a crumpled paper packet of cigarettes.

'When I was a young policeman,' said Flagg significantly, 'I wouldn't have thought of smoking cigarettes when I was driving my superintendent to a murder case. Times have changed. I can see that.'

'It's a fact, Mr. Flagg,' Russell said. 'That's what you call progress. I was nineteen years an' in the army before my old man saw me smoking. Nowadays, the kids puff away in the house like a chimney. Things was a lot better arranged in our young days. I started when I was ten but there's nobody could ever say they saw me doin' it. Everything's altered now.' He sat bolt upright in the driver's seat. 'There's a light or two ahead of us.'

Know All Newall consulted the map. 'This looks like the place—Marchgate Priory.' He peered ahead of him through the blurred windscreen. 'There's the bridge all the talk's about. And the hotel. I won't be sorry to get there, Mr. Flagg. This driving around half the night isn't all it's cracked up to be.'

'It never was,' Flagg said sadly. He shivered in the thin air of morning. 'I'm getting old, Know All. That's what it is. I've seen the day when I'd have walked here just to get my teeth into a good-going case. And I wouldn't have been the only one either. There were men like Carswell and Daly and Mackintosh and Barratt. They're not putting the same sort of stuff into policemen nowadays.'

They drew into the courtyard of the Knight Templar, where a stout, blue-uniformed figure was waiting to receive them. He came forward as the car halted and was in time to open the rear door of it for Flagg. 'Name of Gage, sir,' he said. 'Police Constable Gage. The superintendent is in the Knight, sir, talking to Blane. He's waiting for you.'

They were led in through a long corridor to a small room in which a fire had been lit and breakfast was set. A tall man in a blue suit was engaged in conversation with a pleasant-featured man who was concerning himself with the cutlery. Gage said, 'Superintendent Crayshaw, sir.'

Crayshaw came across and shook hands with Flagg. 'Glad to see you, Inspector.' He indicated his companion. 'This is Peter Blane who'll be responsible for your comfort here. He runs the Knight Templar.'

Blane said: 'We'll do the best we can for you, Inspector. I've got two rooms prepared for you upstairs. We've got a meal ready. I expect you can do with it.' He excused himself, retiring to his own quarters to superintend these operations.

Inspector Newall made a belated appearance, encumbered with two large cases. He laid them down and Flagg crooked a finger at him. 'Come on over here, Know All, and meet Superintendent Crayshaw. Super, this is old Know All. You've probably heard of him yourself. Him that's got the memory all the talk's about.'

Crayshaw had indeed heard of this remarkable policeman for it was a matter of common knowledge that Inspector Newall, unlike the Biblical prophets, was honoured in his own land and particularly so among his own kind. There were few policemen, at least, who had not heard of him, and most of them had met him in the flesh, for Inspector Newall was a great performer at police concerts, benevolent socials, smokers and presentations, where his remarkable talents were much in demand.

In his youth, Newall had appeared on the boards in both London and the provinces, where he was known to all concerned as 'KNOW ALL KNEW ALL—MASTER OF MEMORY', and it was indeed true of him that his powers were at least as phenomenal as the description of them on the billing suggested. Thus, if you were eager to ascertain

66

the precise date of the marriage of Queen Anne, the Battle of Marathon, or the year in which the Jews returned to Jerusalem and began rebuilding the Temple, all that was necessary was to repair to the particular theatre in which this erudite man was appearing, and at the appropriate moment to state your requirements in a loud and clear voice, whereupon satisfaction would be yours forthwith, for, on such items of interest and culture, Noel Newall was a competent authority and had never been found wanting. There were, it is true, scoffers and philistines. There were also those among his colleagues who had attempted upon occasion to trip him up. Certain massive men, particularly among the hierarchy at Central Office, had been known to stay at home o' nights swotting up the kings of Judah, the rivers of Asia, mathematical formulae, and similar like scraps of erudition in foolhardy attempts to confound him and it is a matter of history that all their attempts proved abortive so that they had to retire from the encounter crushed and beaten, their several egos permanently deflated.

Superintendent Flagg had located a comfortable chair. Now he sat down in it. 'We've to have some breakfast, Know All. I'll have a look round and see what's doing here. When you come back we'll get the story from the superintendent.'

Over a gargantuan breakfast he heard as much as Crayshaw was able to tell him, and as was his fashion, he listened to the details without interruption till the superintendent was finished, then: 'What does the doctor say?'

'He was shot once. The bullet went into his brain between his eyes. It came out at the back of his head. Laker says he died as soon as it hit him. The bullet was embedded in the plaster of the inside wall. So far as we can judge it looks like a .38. It's away for examination.'

'And it happened at sometime between seven o'clock and nine?'

67

'So far as we can judge. Probably between seven and eight o'clock. Bentley went out a few minutes before seven. He was missed at eight when he didn't turn up for dinner.'

'What sort of a fellow was he?'

Crayshaw shook his head. 'I didn't know him personally. Gage says he was a very pleasant fellow and very well liked. They've been here almost four years now. Inspector Silver's up at the Close just now taking statements. They're pretty much upset and I suppose the gentlemen will want to get back to London. Do you want to have a word with Gage now? He can give you the picture a bit better than I can, being the man on the spot.'

'We'll have him in,' Flagg said and Police Constable Gage was produced forthwith, a comfortable policeman of the old school, solid, sensible, and unshaken by the horrible happening in his bailiwick. He had been notified of the murder on the previous evening at exactly ten-twenty-seven, which was just as soon as it had been discovered. Clancy and the gardener had come down to the police station to fetch him and he had notified his superiors at once. He gave a clear and factual account of the occurrence, so that by the time Flagg had completed his questioning he had a comprehensive, even a detailed, picture of Marchgate Close, its occupants, and the late lamented Mark Bentley. When the man had finished, he said, 'Would you say Bentley was the sort of man who would make an enemy?'

Gage could not think so. 'I've spoken to him a lot. He was a friendly kind of man and I've never heard of anything against him.'

'What was his line of business?'

'I don't know. He had a bit of money, but he didn't go to any job or anything like that. He kept a fair staff and he ran two or three cars. He always gave to anything in the district that was being collected for.'

'What about his wife?'

'Mrs. Bentley? She's a very pleasant lady, but quiet. She doesn't go about a great deal but she's quite well liked. So is Miss Jane. She's a lot more like Mr. Bentley was—though she's not his own daughter.'

Flagg looked interested. 'What do you mean by that?'

Gage coughed. 'Mrs. Bentley was married before. Mr. Bentley was her second husband. The young lady's father was her first.'

'Where is he now?'

'Somebody said he was dead. I think it was Clancy. He's a kind of manservant. Been with them for years. He's the fellow that can give you the information.'

'Fine,' Flagg said, then dismissed him. He helped himself to more tea, his shrewd blue eyes half closed. He had drunk half of it before he spoke again and when he did it was to Inspector Newall. 'You'd better see if Russell is ready, Know All. We'll probably need to keep him pretty busy.' He peered over at the superintendent. 'Now, Mr. Crayshaw, is there anything else you can think of that might interest us?'

Crayshaw shook his head. 'If there is I can't think of it, Inspector.' He was obviously anxious to be on his way. 'Silver will be waiting for us. He'll give you all the assistance you need.'

Flagg rose, found his voluminous tweed coat and buttoned it high around his neck. 'We'll get away then. You're coming up with us?'

'I am. I'll use my own car and I'll bring Gage up.' He went outside to make the necessary arrangements and by this time Flagg had found his way to the courtyard, where his companions were waiting for him. Crayshaw was in his own car, with Gage beside him. 'We'll get off now. About a couple of miles or so.' The car moved slowly away.

Flagg got into the rear of the car from Central Office, sat back comfortably, and they set off. For a little while they drove in silence, then Flagg said: 'Have a word with this fellow Gage, Know All. He's a sensible kind of man and he may be able to give us an idea or two.'

'He didn't say very much when you were talking to him,' Newall pointed out.

Flagg agreed. 'He didn't. Only facts. I want ideas. But you'll never get ideas from a policeman like Gage when you're talking to him in front of his superior officer. Fellows like Gage don't like to appear clever.'

'That's true,' Russell said. 'You'll never get the best out of a man when his boss is around. I had a word or two with him myself when he came out.'

'Did he tell you anything?'

Russell took a corner with immoderate haste. 'He did indeed, Know All. I've got some 'ighly pleasing information for you both. From what Gage tells me the beer around this place is the best you'll get.'

'That's something,' said Superintendent Flagg and lapsed into a brooding silence.

12

THE superintendent's car led them to the East Lodge and here they made a brief inspection of the scene of the murder. A single constable had been deputed to remain here on guard, and with him they viewed the room in which Mark Bentley's body had been found where, with some solemnity, he pointed out the damage to the plaster occasioned both by the bullet and by its subsequent removal.

'Mr. Silver thinks he must have been sitting in this chair here, sir, when he was shot. There's the mark on the floor where we found him. The inspector made a chalk line round it. The doctor says he was shot from four or five feet range so the murderer was maybe about where you're standing.'

Crayshaw added confirmation of this opinion. 'I don't think there's much doubt but that he was killed here as we've suggested. The only thing that is puzzling is why he came here at all. The place hasn't been used for years.'

This was true. The walls were discoloured with damp, the wallpaper peeling from them and the distemper had flaked from the ceiling leaving it spotted and blotchy. Flagg made a brief survey of the house without gaining much by his inspection. There was the room in which Bentley's body had been found, and it was the largest of three desolate rooms.

They went back out to where the cars were waiting and here Crayshaw added to their knowledge a little. 'This place used to belong to the Venables—an old local family. I think Bentley got it cheaply. These kind of places cost the earth to run and unless you've got a fair income you can do nothing with them.'

The Close came in view as he spoke, a long, two-storied building backed by a walled garden and an imposing array of greenhouses. They swung up the driveway towards the house and Crayshaw got out stiffly. 'You haven't got as much room in here as I have in my car, Mr. Flagg.' He watched Gage bring it up towards the house with a speculative eye. 'I used to think I'd want to spend my life in the Metropolitan Police, but I'm glad now I made the break when I did. It's nice to be a big fish in a small pool. Too much competition in London for the likes of me.'

'There's a lot in what you say,' Flagg said sadly. 'If I were young again I'd start in the country myself. Plenty of eggs and cream and farm butter. The beer's the very best that money can buy and there's hardly any work.'

They went inside. A uniformed constable met them at the door and escorted them through to the study. Here they met Inspector Silver, a lean, capable-looking policeman who was interviewing a girl in the dress of a housemaid. He dismissed her for the moment then came over to shake hands with these new arrivals.

Flagg had looked around for the most comfortable seat. Once he had occupied it he sat back and relaxed. 'Well, here we are, Inspector. I've had an account of the business from the superintendent here, but, of course, you'll have a bit more to tell me.'

Superintendent Crayshaw was obviously in favour of such businesslike sentiments. 'Silver will give you all the assistance he can, Inspector. I'm sure you'll work well together. If there's anything you want—let me know. I'll come round this evening if I can manage and we can talk things over.' He nodded round him and took his departure.

Flagg watched him go. 'That's that, Inspector. What have you got?'

Inspector Silver produced a sheaf of notes. 'I've got most of it down here, sir. I've taken statements from everyone in the house, of course, and I may say that all the statements seem to be fairly straightforward.'

'That's interesting,' Flagg said. He held out a podgy hand. 'I'll have a look through what you've got. In the meantime you might have Newall come in here. I want him to go over these notes with me.'

Newall appeared a moment later and Silver, who knew this erudite man by repute, was pleased to make his personal acquaintance. 'I heard you once at a smoker in Basingstoke, Inspector. Never heard anything like the way you reeled off the Hampshire batting and bowling averages for the last thirty years. A memory like you've got must be a big help to you in your police work. I wish I had it.'

Inspector Newall permitted himself a weary smile.

72

'It's a help all right, Inspector, but there are times when you would just as soon be without it. You've no idea the time I spend keeping out of the way of folk that are always looking for me to answer questions, instead of looking them up in a book. There's a lot of work in in, too. You've got to spend half your time in public libraries swotting up facts and half the people you meet are trying to get you to make a mistake so's they can tell everybody about it.'

'It's a fact,' Flagg said. 'That's the worst of being infallible in your profession. I've been fighting that kind of thing for the last twenty years. Other people trying to pick your brains. Come over here, Know All, and go to work on the inspector's notes.'

For half an hour they sat together poring over the notes and statements Silver had presented for their inspection, and at the end of that time Flagg removed his glasses, rubbed his hands together, and looked at Silver. 'What do you think, Inspector?'

Inspector Silver looked thoughtful. 'I'm not sure what to think so far, Mr. Flagg. These people are all here in the house just now, so you'll be able to have a word with all of them as soon as you like. I expect the men will want to get back to the City as soon as possible.'

'Did they say so?'

'Not in as many words, but it wasn't hard to see how they were feeling.'

'You haven't formed any conclusions of your own?'

'Not yet,' Silver admitted. 'Everybody's shocked. Nobody can think why it should happen to him.'

'There had to be a reason,' Flagg said sagely. 'What does his wife say?'

'She's in bed. The doctor had to come and give her a sedative. I had a word or two with her, but as you can see I didn't get very much. I didn't want to upset the poor woman. She'll probably be able to speak to you later.'

'What about this man Clancy?'

73

'He'll be able to give you more than any of the rest of them,' Silver admitted. 'He's an odd little fellow to find in a country household, but he's been devoted to Bentley.'

'We'll have him in,' Flagg said. He fumbled in his pockets then peered searchingly at the desk where his eye unerringly detected a cigar cutter. He leaned back with a little sigh of satisfaction. Silver had left the room. Now he came back. 'I've sent Gage along to find Clancy, Inspector. If you don't object I'll go along and have a final word with the kitchen staff.'

Clancy made his appearance a moment later, a white-featured woebegone little man whose melancholy aspect bore evidence of his distress. He came in almost furtively, looked from Flagg to Newall then back again. ''Mornin', gents. The inspector said you wanted to see me. 'Ere I am. Do anythin' you ask if it'll 'elp.'

'Fine,' Flagg said. He studied the little man with shrewd appraising eyes. It was obvious that Clancy looked upon the death of Mark Bentley as a tragedy, equally obvious that he regarded it as a personal tragedy. 'You've been with Mr. Bentley for a long time, Clancy?'

'Twenty-one years,' Clancy said. 'But I knew Mark before that, maybe four or five. I even worked with 'im a bit. One of the best. No side—nothin' of that sort. Mr. B was a gentleman. I did for him for a spell before 'e got married to Mrs. B. I was away for a while—then I came back.'

'You got on well with him?'

Clancy laid a forefinger and a middle finger on the desk top. 'Him an' me was just like that,' he said impressively. 'Many a good night we 'ad together when Mrs. B was away. Old Mark didn't think nothin' of sitting down for a game of banker or a hand at nap. We couldn't 'ave got along better.'

'Tell me about it,' Flagg said. He patted absent-mindedly at his pockets, going over them all in turn. When he spoke again there was exasperation in his voice.

'What do you know, Inspector? I've come out without my cigars. There they were, lying on the kitchen table when I was getting ready to leave. I can mind fine the wife saying, "Don't forget your cigar-case whatever you do, or you'll have nothing to smoke till you get back"— and here I am without it.'

Inspector Newall was prepared to be helpful. 'Maybe I could give her a ring, Mr. Flagg. She could send them on and you'd get them tomorrow.'

Flagg regarded him coldly. 'Like as not she'd miss the post and here I would be without a smoke till Monday at the earliest.'

Clancy stepped into the breach. 'Beggin' your pardon, sir, maybe I could 'elp. Mr. Mark always kept a box of cigars for visitors.' He went across to a little bureau, opened a drawer and produced a cabinet. ' 'Ere you are, Superintendent.'

Flagg's predatory instincts were aroused. 'I'll take one or two, Clancy, just to keep me going.' He put half a dozen in his pocket, then selected another from the box. 'The inspector here doesn't smoke cigars. It's an easy round.' He struck a match, puffed away in silence for a moment or so. 'That's something like the thing. Now we'll get down to business, Clancy. You and Mr. Bentley were great pals you were saying. That means you'd likely be pretty much in his confidence.'

'About some things,' Clancy said cautiously. ' 'E didn't talk about everything.'

'Have you got any idea who shot him?'

Clancy looked vicious. 'I got no idea, Inspector. If I did I'd let you know. I wouldn't give a damn who it was either if it was his nearest an' dearest.'

Flagg took the cigar out of his mouth. 'How did Bentley get along with his wife?'

'Pretty well. Old Mark thought the world of 'er. Do anythin' to make 'er 'appy.'

'That's nice. What did she think of him?'

75

'I don't know, sir. They never quarrelled or anythin' like that. She don't show her feelin's like Mark did, but I think she was just as fond of him.'

'She'd been married before?'

'Twenty years ago an' more,' Clancy said.

'What happened to her first husband?'

'Died, they tells me. Out abroad someplace. They was divorced. It was a while after that before 'e died. I can't tell you about 'im. I never saw the gent.'

'What about the daughter?'

'Miss Jane? She's as nice a young lady as you could find.'

'How did she get along with her stepfather?'

'They was quite good pals,' Clancy said. 'She got on better with Mark than she did with her own mother. Mark thought a lot of 'er. I've often 'eard 'im say so, but she 'as a mind of 'er own.'

'What about these two gentlemen who are staying with you just now?'

'Mr. Verrall is the lawyer,' Clancy said. 'Been comin' about the place for years now. Mr. Selwyn is an old pal of Mr. B's. Mr. Selwyn don't come quite so often now. He was in America for a long time.'

'Did you ever hear Mr. Bentley say he had any enemies of any sort?'

Clancy shook his head. 'I never did. Old Mark wasn't the feller to 'ave enemies.'

'Who do you think murdered him, then?'

Clancy looked startled. 'Who do I think? So far I ain't 'ad a chance to think. I've been too busy. Up all night, an' the shock of it all.'

Flagg looked him over shrewdly. 'What you need is a drop of whisky to pull you together. Is there anything handy?'

Clancy brightened visibly. 'It's a good idea.' He went over to a little cabinet, produced a decanter.

'Will you look at that, Superintendent? The laziness

of the women in this 'ouse is beyond redemption. If I don't do a thing it ain't done.'

Flagg looked up. 'What is it?'

'Dirty glasses,' Clancy said in disgust. 'Left lyin' there since last night. There's the glasses old Verrall an' poor old Mark used. I'll take 'em with me.'

'Forget them,' Flagg said pointedly and the little man was prepared to do so for the moment.

'Will you 'ave a little drop, gents? It's early in the day but we're all in need of somethin'.'

Flagg shook his head. 'Not for us, Clancy. In the Force it don't do. Somebody would smell it on your breath and put in a report and then where's your reputation? But you have a drink for yourself. Was Mr. Bentley worried about anything recently? Did he strike you as having anything on his mind?'

Clancy swallowed his whisky. 'He was just the same as he always was, except that he was a bit upset when I saw 'im last.'

Flagg tapped the sheet of paper in front of him. 'It says here he seemed a bit upset. You told Inspector Silver that. So did the young lady. What upset him?'

Clancy shrugged. 'Search me, Superintendent. Old Mark didn't speak to me at all. I didn't speak to 'im. You could always tell when 'e was upset an' when 'e was the best thing to do was to keep out of the way. I said nothin'.'

'And had he been in his usual kind of mood all day?'

'Right up till six o'clock. There or thereabouts. One time I saw 'im 'e was fine. Next time 'e passed me without lookin' at me an' a face like thunder.'

Flagg said, 'That was after Mr. Selwyn came, wasn't it?'

Clancy's eyes grew narrow. 'That's right, Superintendent. But I don't think that 'ad anythin' to do with it, for——'

'Maybe not,' Flagg said cheerfully. 'I'm just curious.

Let me see your hands, Clancy. Over here to the light with them.'

The little man laid down the glass, his eyes suddenly startled. He walked over to the window to which Flagg had made his way. For a moment the policeman examined his hands, back and front, then he grunted. 'That should do just now, Clancy.' He led him over to the door. 'The inspector tells me these gentlemen want to get back to London. I'll see them now. You send in the lawyer fellow right away.' He opened the door. 'You can round up Selwyn in a minute or two for me. Know All—go along with Clancy and have a word in the kitchen.'

Inspector Newall rose, a little surprised. 'Just now, Mr. Flagg?'

'Just now,' Flagg said. 'Clancy, take the inspector along with you.' He stood by the door until they had gone out, then closed it quietly behind them.

13

A FIRE had been lit in the large and comfortable morning-room, and over it sat Johnny Selwyn. Verrall stood by the window peering out at the police cars which occupied the driveway immediately in front of the house, his rather lined face a shade more haggard than usual. Jane sat beside the fire.

'I wish these infernal policemen would get on with the job,' Selwyn said irritably. 'Can't you go along and hurry them a bit, Verrall?'

Mr. Verrall turned round slowly. 'The police move in their own time, I'm afraid.'

Johnny screwed up his eyes. 'I could do with a sleep myself. I'll bet you could too, Jane. Why don't you go up and lie down?'

'I couldn't. I don't want to sleep, Johnny. I want to do something. Can't you understand that?'

He looked at her curiously. 'I suppose you do, Jane. I think we all do. Poor old Mark. It's Faith I'm sorry for. How is she now?'

'She was sleeping half an hour ago,' Jane said. 'Dr. Lee gave her some tablets. She didn't want to take them but he insisted on it.' She jumped to her feet. 'I'd better go upstairs again. If they send for me you can ask Dyer to come up. I'll sit beside her for a while.' She left the room and in the hallway met Clancy and a tall, lean man with melancholy eyes and a blue chin. Clancy halted her.

'This is Inspector Newall, miss. Gent from Scotland Yard.'

She looked at Newall with some interest. 'Do you want to see me?'

Inspector Newall shook his head. 'Not for the moment, miss. Superintendent Flagg will want a word with you before long. A dreadful business.'

'Indeed it is. It's all so—so incomprehensible. Inspector Silver says it can't be anything else but murder. Somehow I can hardly believe that. Nobody would want to murder Mark.'

'Somebody did.'

She bit at her lip. 'But couldn't it have been an accident?'

'You don't get that kind of accident, miss. There had been a car there. It looks as though Mr. Bentley had arranged to meet someone there secretly—and this party had come prepared to murder him.'

She shivered. 'How horrible!' She looked at Clancy. 'I'm going up to see Mummy. If you need me, Clancy, I'll be up there. You can send someone up.' She left them and made her way to the bedroom above, with all the sensations of someone living through a nightmare. It was impossible to believe that Mark Bentley was dead.

She reached the door of the bedroom—and opened it very gently. The curtains had been drawn but a pale silver light, which was not unpleasant, filtered into the room. Faith Bentley lay very still. She was facing the window, but her eyes were closed. Dyer, the maid, sat in a low armchair, knitting methodically in the semi-darkness. Now she looked up.

'Has she wakened yet?'

The woman shook her head. 'I hope she keeps on sleeping. A terrible shock it has been to everyone, but to her more than anybody. I don't know whether I'm on my head or my heels, myself.'

Jane sat down. 'You'd better slip down to the kitchen, Dyer, and have some tea. I'll wait here till you come back.'

The woman rose readily enough. 'I won't be any longer than I can help, miss. An awful business. I never knew the like.' It was easy to see that she was eager for information and with all the latent curiosity of her class was prepared to derive a certain vicarious pleasure from her proximity to sudden and violent death. 'Have the police gentlemen been able to find out anything yet, miss?'

'I haven't had a chance to ask them,' Jane said coldly.

Dyer sighed. 'And I doubt if they'd tell you if you did. Very artful crowd these here policemen, miss. When Dyer was alive he would have no truck with them at all.' She slipped out quietly, closing the door behind her as she did so.

For a moment or so the girl sat in silence, then she heard her mother say, 'Jane, has Dyer gone now?'

She rose and went over to the bed. 'Yes, Mummy, I sent her down to have some tea.' She sat down on the edge of the bed. 'I didn't know you had wakened. How do you feel now?'

80

Faith Bentley shivered. 'Ghastly. Poor Mark. It's impossible to think about. Absolutely impossible. What was Dyer saying about the police before she went out?'

'She was saying her husband hadn't liked them.'

'As if it mattered, Jane. Get me a drink of something. I feel positively wretched and I suppose these horrible men will be wanting to talk to me about it. Have you seen them yet?'

'I've seen the inspector who came out from Reading. There are some more men from London now.'

The older woman shivered. 'It's ghastly. I don't know how I can bear to speak to them about Mark. And to think I was so unpleasant to him, too.' She began to weep.

Jane became practical. 'I don't think you should dwell on that, Mummy. I think you should have some tea. I'll go down and fetch some.'

'No, don't go, Jane. Don't leave me alone. Stay here and talk to me. Have the others left yet? Is Johnny Selwyn still here?'

'They're both in the morning-room.'

'What do they think about it?'

Jane said wearily: 'What could anyone think about it? Everybody's completely at their wits' end. Mr. Verrall keeps on saying it must have been an accident but Johnny doesn't believe it was. I hope Mr. Verrall is right, but—but——'

There was the sound of the door handle turning. Faith said: 'That must be Dyer coming back. Don't let her know I'm waken, Jane. I simply couldn't bear to discuss it with her.'

Mrs. Dyer came in on tiptoe.

'How is she, my dear?'

'I think she'll be all right if she can just rest. Dr. Lee said he would come back before lunch time. If she could sleep till then it would be a help.' She went quietly over to the door. 'I'll go downstairs now, Dyer. There must be something I can do down there to help. Where's Clancy?'

Clancy had been in the lower hall when Dyer had come up. Jane made her way to his retreat without delay, where she found Clancy, an agitated man, smoking a cigarette. 'Come in, Miss Jane. Did you want somethin'?'

'I want to find out what's been happening, Clancy.'

The little man blew a cloud of smoke. 'The superintendent feller's got old Verrall in there just now, for all the good it will do him.'

'What is he like, this Superintendent Flagg?'

'A big fat feller.' He licked his lips. 'They say he's a pretty smart policeman. Mr. Selwyn's heard quite a lot about him.' He looked at her moodily. 'It'll be your turn next. I've 'ad mine for the time bein'.'

'What was it like?'

He shrugged his thin shoulders. 'Like what you'd expect. Questions an' more questions. You would think they'd get fed up askin' 'em.'

'I suppose that's the only way they can find out anything.' She looked down at his thin, pinched face in silence for a moment or so, then: 'Clancy, what do you think it all means? Why do you think he was murdered?'

The little man licked his lips. 'God knows, Miss Jane.'

'You haven't got any ideas about it?'

He shivered. 'Not me. You know me, miss. Would I be sittin' here like this if I 'ad any ideas about it?'

'I don't know. I hope not. But these things don't just happen. They happen because somebody meant them to happen. They happen because somebody wanted them to happen, Clancy. You knew Mark better than anyone alive. Who was it?'

'I can't tell you that.'

'You're not just saying that? You're not just covering up? Tell me the truth, Clancy. I've got to know.'

He looked surprised at the vehemence in her voice.

'You get an 'old of yourself, Miss Jane. We got plenty on our minds without you being upset next.'

She knew that her moment, of near-hysteria was past. 'I'm sorry, Clancy. I didn't mean to upset you.' She slid from the table, still watching him. 'It's all so horrible, isn't it? Just to think Mark's gone. Just to think we'll never see him again.' She went over to the door. 'We're going to have to stick together on this business, Clancy, because Mummy won't be much use.'

'That's right, miss. We'll do that.'

She hesitated for one moment, then, turning, went back into the corridor and along to the hall. In the Great Hall itself a lean, blue-clad figure was examining an oil-painting which hung above the wide fireplace. He turned towards her as she approached and she recognized the melancholy figure of Inspector Newall. He raised a large, bony hand in salutation. 'Well, miss, here we are again. You've got some fine paintings here. I was just admiring that one above the fire there.' He indicated it with a careless nod. 'It's a great favourite of mine, depicting, as it does, the well-known and highly celebrated Trojan Horse. There was a caper for you if you like. And it all began because a lady didn't know she was well off where she was. You'll remember that, of course, when Helen, the wife of Menelaus, King of Sparta, pushed off with Paris, the son of Priam, King of Troy. A first-class bit of scandal that must have been at the time.'

'I suppose so,' she said. She was a little dazed. A policeman with even a nodding acquaintance with the legendary figures of Greek mythology was a somewhat startling phenomenon. 'I didn't think that Scotland Yard officers would have a great deal of time for stories of that sort.'

Inspector Newall smiled a deprecatory smile. 'On the whole they haven't, miss. Being in the Force doesn't give you much time for culture, as it were. Between you and me, the ignorance of the average detective is a national scandal and I've been saying that for years now. Mind you, they're kept busy all right, but even the busiest of them should have time for a bit of reading. But how many of them get round to it? I wouldn't like to say. Ask the average detective at Central Office who wrote the *Areopagitica* and he would think you were making fun of him. Mention the *Wealth of Nations*, or Boswell's *Life of Johnson* and he wouldn't know if he was on his head or his heels. And that's only one angle of it. There's plenty others: mathematics, science, foreign languages, or geography. Take a simple thing like history. Who was the first President of the French Republic? When I was at school it was Louis Adolph Thiers. After him was Marshal MacMahon and then Jules Grévy. The first President of America was the far-famed George Washington, as all the world knows. He was the fellow who chopped down the cherry tree and could not tell a lie about it. After him came John Adams and the first Republican, Thomas Jefferson.'

She looked at him curiously. 'I didn't know you needed to know all that sort of thing to be a policeman.'

There was the sound of a telephone ringing as she spoke. The girl started. 'That's from the study, Inspector.'

'I'll attend to it,' Newall said. He walked along to the study door and went inside. A moment more and he reappeared, crooking a finger towards her. 'For you, miss. It's a gentleman. He didn't give his name but——'

She was staring at him, grey-faced, ashen. She came slowly towards him, then, as she did so, the world started to whirl about her as though revolving on a central axis. She staggered forward; the light of day left her eyes and the strong arms of Inspector Newall caught her as she fell.

84

14

FLAGG threw wide the door of the study. 'Bring her in here, Know All.'

The inspector carried the girl inside. There was a small sofa underneath the windows. He laid her on this and Superintendent Flagg produced a glass with considerable promptitude. 'Give her this.' He went back to where Johnny Selwyn stood, a harassed witness of all that had happened.

'All right, Mr. Selwyn, you can go now. I don't think we'll need you any longer.'

Johnny rose, more than a little perturbed. 'What about Jane, Superintendent? Can't I get some help or something? I'll telephone the doctor and——'

'She's fainted,' Flagg said. 'That's all. The doctor couldn't do any more if he was here on the spot.' He walked across to the telephone, lifted the receiver and held it to his ear. 'Hullo, hullo? Anybody there?' For a moment or so he stood there. 'Hung up,' he said significantly. 'Well, that can't be helped. If he wants her he can try again.' He laid the receiver down and went over to where Inspector Newall was bending over the girl. 'Colour's coming back, Know All. You'll see her open her eyes in a minute.' He went over to the door. 'Come now, Mr. Selwyn. The young lady's in good hands. She couldn't be in better. The inspector and me will take as good care of her as you would yourself.'

Selwyn went out, albeit reluctantly. 'I'll send one of the maids along, Flagg. She'll probably want to go and lie down, you know.'

'She's lying down,' Flagg said. 'My guess is she'll want to get up. Good morning, Mr. Selwyn. I don't think we'll need to keep you around any longer now.'

'I don't want to go back to London.'

Flagg considered him gravely. 'Maybe not. You'd better take that up with Mrs. Bentley. But so far as I'm concerned you're at liberty to go whenever you want.' He closed the door then crossed over to where Inspector Newall was propping up the girl's head. She had opened her eyes now, and colour was coming back into her cheeks. She sipped slowly at the whisky, then:

'What happened? Did I faint?'

'You fainted,' said Flagg romantically. 'Right into old Know All's arms. It was as neat a thing as ever I saw. You would think you'd rehearsed it for a month. You're Miss Jane Bentley, I understand. I'm Flagg. Superintendent Flagg.'

'Of course.' She looked into the shrewd blue eyes, the rugged, seamed features. Flagg was large and grossly fat, his features heavy and fleshy, crossed and criss-crossed with a thousand little lines of care, experience, grimness, and among them those which hinted at good humour and humanity—a respect for his fellow men and an understanding for their frailties and foibles. She liked him instinctively. Now he laid down the glass.

'You all right now, miss?'

'Yes. I feel a good bit better.'

'You'll feel better still in a minute or two. Inspector, you slip out and get the young lady some tea.' He watched Newall leave, a little twinkle in his heavy-lidded eyes. 'Never saw old Know All in a flap like that before,' he said conversationally. 'You gave us all a bit of a start —including Mr. Selwyn. He's a friend of yours, I can see?'

'He was a friend of Mark's.' There was a little inflection in her voice which he did not fail to notice.

Flagg shook his head. 'He was worried about my not being able to handle a young woman in a faint. Little does he know! I've got seven daughters of my own—I'm a dab hand at faints of every shape and form. When I was

86

at Acton the neighbours came to me instead of going to the doctor for things like teething, measles, mumps and colic. Those were the days.' He went over to his own chair and sat down in it. 'Well, I'm glad you're here, miss. I was just about to send for you, when the 'phone rang. It was a coincidence in a way. Who was he?'

'I don't know. The inspector didn't say.'

'He didn't know either,' Flagg said. 'I heard him ask. It's unusual, miss. And in a murder case we like to know as much as we can about everybody we can. It's not just nosiness. It's a part of the general picture. Did you expect a telephone call?'

'No. I didn't expect one.'

Flagg rubbed at his cheek. 'We'll find out,' he said cheerfully. 'Now I think I hear old Know All coming with the tea.' The door opened as he spoke. Inspector Newall came in, bearing a large silver tray, three cups and the usual appurtenances of tea. 'You couldn't have come at a better time. I'll pour out, Know All. You get on the telephone and check that incoming call to Miss Bentley here.'

Newall went over and sat down in front of the table. Flagg lifted a teaspoon. 'Sugar, Miss Bentley? There you go—I'll stir it for you.'

She drank the tea in silence, and felt much the better for it. Flagg had relit his cigar. 'It's a sad business this, Miss Bentley, and I'm afraid we're going to have to ask you to give us a lot of your time and attention.'

'Of course, Mr. Flagg. I'll be glad to do that.'

'It means asking a lot of questions, and some of them you're maybe not going to like very much. Even if you don't—they've still got to be answered.'

'Yes. I can understand that.'

'That's good, miss. You'd be surprised at the number of people who don't.'

For half an hour by the clock he questioned her,

87

seeking, probing, for some sort of lead or for some information which might be likely to supply one. At the end of that time he sat back, surveying her moodily. 'That's that, miss. We won't have to keep you a great deal longer. Do you think Mrs. Bentley would be well enough to answer a few questions? We'll have to get a statement from her.'

'I was with her before I came here. She's still pretty much upset.'

'It's got to be done,' Flagg said. 'I'll have a word with the doctor when he comes along. Clancy says he's to be back before twelve. Clancy seems quite an important fellow in this household so far as I can see.'

'He's been here all his life.'

'He told me that. He was a great friend of your step-father's.'

'Yes. Mark was fond of him. Mark left everything to Clancy.'

'Well, we've covered a fair amount, miss. There's one or two points I'm hazy on yet. What was Mr. Bentley's line? What did he make his money out of?'

'I don't really know. We've always been pretty well off as long as I can remember. I think he must have had a lot of money invested abroad. He used to go away quite a lot on business trips, though he hasn't been away so much since we came here to live. Before that he used to be away a good deal—especially when I was at school. I used to get postcards and letters with all sorts of wonderful stamps on them, and I swopped them with the other girls.'

'And you've never heard him talking business?'

She shook her head decidedly. 'No. Mark didn't approve very much of girls going out to work and he didn't like them to be interested in business. But Mr. Verrall will be able to tell you. He's done Mark's business for years now. Haven't you seen him yet?'

88

'I have,' Flagg said. 'He was able to give me quite a bit of help.' He regarded her thoughtfully. 'Mr. Bentley was your mother's second husband, they tell me?'

'Yes.' For a moment she thought he was about to pursue that particular line of questioning. Instead he switched to another.

'Now, miss, this is maybe a little bit personal, but it's the sort of thing a policeman has to ask. How did you get on with Mr. Bentley?'

'Very well indeed. I was very fond of him.'

He took the cigar out of his mouth, tossed it into the fire, and said regretfully: 'That was a good smoke. It's a pity they don't last long. Well, there's not much more. Maybe just this. How did Mr. Bentley and your mother get along together?'

'Very well. They were ideally matched. Mark adored Mummy and did everything he could think of to please her. Why do you ask that?'

'It's just one of the questions,' he said. 'Routine, miss —like what's your name and what were you doing between a quarter to seven and a quarter past seven last night? And while we're on the subject, what were you doing?'

'What was I doing?' She thought for a moment. 'Nothing in particular. I talked to Johnny for a few moments, then I read a magazine article for a while. After that I had a bath and got dressed for dinner.'

'Where did you spend your time then, Miss Bentley?'

'Mostly in my own bedroom I should say—and in the bathroom.'

Flagg sighed. 'A pity. Everybody seems to have been on his lonesome at that particular time. Clancy was in his room decanting port and having a smoke. Mrs. Bentley was lying down, Mr. Selwyn was in his room and after that in the morning-room for a spell. Mr. Verrall was here. He waited here till about twenty minutes after seven and then went to tidy up. Nobody can vouch for

anybody else for that half hour. That makes it awkward.'
His voice hardened. 'It makes it something else.'

She felt a little stab of apprehension. 'What do you
mean, Superintendent.

'I mean,' Flagg said, 'that the murderer picked a nice
handy time to do the job. You would almost have thought
he knew the run of the house.' He beamed down at her.
'Well, we'll see. We've got a long way to go yet. You
can go now, miss.'

'Thank you, Superintendent. And I'll find out about
Mummy from Dr. Lee.'

'Good,' said Flagg and closed the door behind
her.

Inspector Newall helped himself to a cigarette from a
limp cardboard packet, lit it then peered curiously at his
large superior. 'What do you think, Mr. Flagg?'

'Where did the 'phone call come from?'

'From a telephone kiosk about a mile from the house.
The operator couldn't say who had put through the call,
though.'

Flagg grunted. 'It was a man.'

'It was a man all right,' Newall conceded. 'But I doubt
if I'd know his voice if I heard it again. He asked for
Miss Jane Bentley. I told him to hold on.'

The superintendent sighed. 'She was half expecting a
call,' he said shrewdly, 'and she keeled over when she
got it. Was that because we'd taken it, I wonder?'

Newall looked startled. 'You could never prove that.'

Superintendent Flagg chuckled softly. 'There's a lot
of things in this world that you can never prove, Know
All, but it don't prevent them looking very interesting.'
He took something from the desk at his hand. 'Here's
something different. You can get a "yes" or "no" on it
right away. Get it off to Carmody at once. Silver will give
you a motor-cycle policeman.'

Newall took the little parcel gingerly. 'What is it?'

'Whisky glasses,' Flagg said. 'Clancy's prints are on one

90

of them. I'm wondering if there could maybe happen to be anyone else's prints about. You never know your luck. On your way, Know All.'

15

CLANCY was in the main hall when Jane Bentley came out of the study, and he waited for her to approach him.

'Old Verrall,' he said significantly. 'Goin' back to London right away. He wants to see you first.'

'What about Mr. Selwyn?'

'Sittin' in the morning-room,' Clancy said. 'I asked 'im what he meant to do. I think 'e'll stay for a while. That was what 'e said.' He dropped his voice to a conspiratorial whisper. 'What did they say to you in there?'

'Just asked more questions.' She left him and went along to locate Verrall. He was talking to Selwyn when she appeared and he came towards her at once.

'Clancy says you're going back to London, Mr. Verrall?'

'Yes. I think that will be most suitable. Mark's death is going to mean a considerable amount of work for me and I want to tackle it as soon as possible.' He raised one hand to Johnny and led her from the room. 'Now, young lady, this is all going to be very difficult. In some ways I wish I could wait over the week-end at least, but unfortunately that would not do at all. However, Selwyn has agreed to remain here and——'

'But why should he?'

He looked a little surprised. 'Don't you think it better there should be a man in the house at a time like this,

Jane?' There was something so spinsterish in his voice that she smiled in spite of herself.

'I hardly think it necessary. There are plenty of policemen—and Clancy is always here. I'm not frightened, if that's what you have in mind, Mr. Verrall.' She walked with him out into the hall. 'I'll have Clancy bring your car round.'

'It's already here,' he said. 'A deplorable business, Jane. However, there is nothing we can do about that now. Nothing but lend assistance to the police and help in any way that is possible. If you require me—don't hesitate to get on the telephone. Over the week-end I expect to have things tidied up to some extent, but—' he spread out his hands—'it will not be the easiest of tasks.' He had opened the door now; the girl followed him out to the broad step.

'Mr. Verrall, there is one question I would like to ask you.'

'What is that?'

'What sort of business was Mark in? How did he make his money?'

He looked at her in some surprise. 'Most of his income came from investments, Jane. He had quite a fair amount tied up abroad. Recently things have not been going so well for him—but of course there is still a sound income. Your mother will be a comparatively wealthy woman. I am not quite certain how wealthy.' He patted her on the shoulder. 'Now I must go, Jane. You should not wait here—it's cold.' He raised his hat, went down the steps towards the car which had been drawn up before the house. She went inside, closing the door, heard the car pull away as she went back down the hall.

Johnny Selwyn was standing by the fire when she went back to the morning-room. He waved her in as she appeared. 'Come and sit down. Tell me what's happened.'

She hesitated, then dropped to the arm of a chair. 'Not very much, Johnny. Mr. Verrall was saying you meant to

92

wait for a few days. It's nice of you, Johnny, but you don't really need to do that.'

'I don't suppose I do need to do it. But I'd rather like to.' He looked at her steadily. 'If you don't want me to wait—if you feel I'll be a nuisance or anything like that —say so. I can slip away at almost any old time. It's up to you, and to Faith.'

She thought it over. 'I'll speak to Mummy about it. But we can't have you waiting just because you feel someone has to be here.' She jumped up as she spoke. 'Now I'm going up to see her. Superintendent Flagg wants to talk to her.'

'Is she fit enough for that?'

'She'll have to be, won't she?'

'I suppose so, but Faith's a highly strung sort of person and the police can be pretty terrifying.'

'They weren't in the least terrifying to me. I thought the superintendent was rather nice.'

'Flagg?' He was a little amused. 'Capable, I suppose. He didn't strike me as being particularly nice. Just the same, they couldn't have put a better man on the job.'

'Do you know him, Johnny?'

'I don't know him. I know of him. Flagg's got a reputation. He's sent a lot of men to the gallows in his day. He's one of the smartest men at the Yard.'

'Is he?' She walked over to the door. 'Now I must go. I've got to see Mummy—and the doctor. You'll excuse me, Johnny.' She went down the hall. Clancy was dusting the heavy gilt frame of a painting which adorned the wall. Now he leaned over towards her.

'The superintendent's gone up to see Mrs. B. The police doctor came in a moment or two ago. They've gone up together.'

She eyed him uncertainly. 'I suppose they have to see her.'

Clancy nodded emphatically. 'No way out of that, miss.'

She left him and made her way through to the rear of the house, slipped on a long rainproof, and went out. There was an odd sense of fear at her heart—which had been present with her since the murdered body of Mark had been found. In itself it postulated a question and it was a question which she had to answer. She went down to the stables, got out her bicycle, climbed on to it, and cycled down the driveway. There was a uniformed policeman standing at the West Lodge and he opened the gate for her, waved her on, then closed it after she had gone out. There were one or two cars on the road, and across from the main gate a little knot of people. She saw one or two of them look towards her, then a tall man in a grey tweed coat came over towards her. 'Good morning, miss. Are you going to the village? If you are—I'd advise you to go by car. There are two or three reporters here. It might not do any harm to avoid them for a day or so.'

She looked at him a little nervously. 'Thank you. Who are you?'

'Detective Constable Merry, miss. My opinion is these chaps may well recognize you and follow you into Marchgate Priory. It isn't worth while taking a chance on.'

'I'll risk it,' she said grimly. She got back on to her bicycle and pedalled away. Once or twice she looked back, but the road behind her was bare of traffic, and she came into the village of Marchgate Priory without having been molested. She turned into the courtyard of the Knight Templar and went into the house.

A maid was in the back corridor when she went through, and the girl looked up in some surprise.

'Miss Jane.' She came towards her. 'Oh, Miss Jane, we were all so upset to hear the news. Poor Mr. Bentley! I'm so sorry about it.'

She said: 'Thank you, Linda. Is Mr. Blane here?'

'I don't know, miss. I haven't seen him all morning. I'll go along to the bar and find out.'

'I'll be upstairs,' Jane said. She made her way above

94

to Peter Blane's private room, and here she dropped into the large armchair, limp and exhausted, her brain aching with weariness. She could have been sitting there for no more than a minute when she heard footsteps coming along the passage towards her. There was a tap at the door, then the girl looked in.

'Mr. Blane isn't in the building just now, miss. Polly says he went away in the Hillman about an hour ago. She thought he took the Reading road.'

Jane looked at her blankly. 'And you don't know when he'll be back?'

'No, miss. He didn't say anything about going away, and with these policemen from London he'll want to be in the house.'

She looked up, puzzled. 'Policemen from London? Are they here?'

'Yes, Miss Jane. A big fat man called Superintendent Flagg and two other ordinary-looking ones. They're on the first floor.'

She put thoughts of Superintendent Flagg and his colleagues out of her mind. Peter Blane she had to see without delay. She said: 'I've got to get back home at once, Linda, but I'll leave a note for Mr. Blane. Will you tell him I've called?'

'Yes, of course, miss. You write your note and I'll see he gets it when he comes back. Leave it on the desk and he can't miss it.' She went out and Jane crossed to the desk. She lifted a sheet of paper from the rack, stared at it for a moment, then wrote:

Peter,
    I must see you as soon as possible. Please don't try to telephone. I shan't be able to come down but can you manage to meet me tonight? It's desperately important. If you can get up I'll meet you at the Trysting Tree at nine o'clock. I can't wait for long, so please be on time.
                                            Jane

She read over what she had written, placed it in an envelope, and wrote across the front of it: *Peter Blane Esq.* She sealed the envelope, propped it up on the desk, then went downstairs. A moment more and she was on her bicycle and had crossed the bridge, with Marchgate Priory and the Knight Templar falling behind her, conscious of the fact that her problem was still unsolved and that the grey dread of doubt still shadowed her. For five minutes she pedalled, then she saw a car approaching her at high speed. A second more and it had passed. She dropped her head as it did so, but not far enough, nor quickly enough, to escape the vigilant eye of Inspector Newall. 'The young lady from the Big House,' he said informatively. 'I wonder where she's been off to, Russell?'

Police Constable Russell, an unsubtle soul, sighed. 'What's the odds, Know All? You want me to drop you at the hotel?'

'I do,' said Inspector Newall, and prepared himself to clamber out. For one moment he stood on the gravelled driveway in front of the Knight Templar, then raised a hand in salute. 'Give my regards to Mr. Carmody, Russell. And be back here as smart as you can. Those were Mr. Flagg's very words.'

'Trust me,' said Russell, and let out the clutch.

16

IT WAS late afternoon when Superintendent Flagg returned to the hotel, a weary man, and when he arrived there the indefatigable Inspector Newall was writing out reports at a small desk. He looked up as his superior officer came into the room. 'We expected you a while ago, Mr. Flagg. I had my lunch by myself.'

Flagg peeled off his coat. 'It's beer I want,' he said. 'I had lunch at the Close. Me and Silver. Ring the bell, Know All, and see about some beer.'

Newall was more than willing to oblige. With a large tankard in front of him, Superintendent Flagg relaxed sufficiently to light a cigar. 'This Mark Bentley knew a a good cigar when he saw one. I'll say that for him.' He puffed pleasantly.

Newall watched him shrewdly. 'What do you think of them all, Mr. Flagg?'

Flagg shrugged. 'What can you think as early as this? Their stories all hang together so far but we haven't tried to pull them apart. I had a look over Bentley's papers with Silver. There was nothing at all that was that interesting. So there you go. Nobody saw anything or heard anything that could help the police. I'm hoping Carmody may have something. It would always be a start.'

'You think Clancy might have a record?'

Flagg sighed. 'What do you think, Know All?'

Inspector Newall considered. 'He's a bit of a rough diamond, but lots of gentlemen pick up a customer like that. The girl was in the village. We met her on the way down. Riding a bike, too.'

Superintendent Flagg was interested. 'Riding a bike, eh? I wonder where she was?'

'Here. I asked the maid about her. She's friendly with Blane. It seems there's quite a bit of talk about it. They didn't like it at the Close.' He told Flagg the gist of what he had learned by careful questioning, and the superintendent was intrigued.

'Fancy that now. A nice young lady. Blane looks a bit old for her, but you never can tell. Which maid did you get all this from?'

'The thin one,' Newall said. 'Name of Edith. The

trouble is you can never tell how much of it is true and how much just say so. Somebody coming along the corridor, Mr. Flagg.'

There was a knock on the door as he spoke. It was Inspector Silver, and the local man came in rubbing his hands. 'Getting colder, Mr. Flagg. My guess is we'll have snow and then we'll have fun.'

Flagg received him hospitably. 'Sit down, Inspector, and have some beer. Not a better thing you could drink when you've got a lot of brain work in hand. Know All, get the inspector something to drink and we'll have a conference.'

With a tankard at his hand, Silver was prepared to relax a little. 'This is what I'm needing. I've been on the job since midnight and I'm beginning to feel it. It's a queer business. Bentley was a well-liked and highly popular man. Nobody seems to be able to imagine he could have had an enemy at all. These people are all his friends and none of them—not even his wife—can give us the slightest help. The one thing we do know is that he went down to the East Lodge to meet some-body. But who was that somebody? Was it a man or a woman?'

Flagg considered his cigar. 'What do you think?'

'I don't know. It seems pretty queer to me he didn't mention it to any of the rest of them.'

'Maybe he did.'

Silver's eyes narrowed. 'You think somebody knew? If that's the case, then, one of them is lying. That helps a bit.'

The big man laughed softly. 'I didn't say that. But maybe they have their own ideas. They won't help you much till you go to work on them. That's been my ex-perience of these kind of cases. What do you say about it, Know All?'

Inspector Newall was in complete agreement. 'The chances are somebody knows or somebody suspects.

98

Bentley must have made an arrangement to meet the murderer. What puzzles me is that nobody else knew anything about it. He didn't mention this meeting to anybody. He left Verrall, to go out and get knocked, without dropping even a hint he had a job on hand that might be dangerous. Why was that?'

Flagg beamed. 'I was wondering when you were going to come to that, Know All. This little private meeting was so secret he didn't mention it to anyone—and yet he got knocked. Then it looks like Bentley didn't expect to get knocked when he went out. What do you make of it?'

Inspector Silver looked puzzled. 'What I make of it is that the man he went out to meet was a lot more dangerous than Bentley expected.'

'That's right,' Flagg said. 'A lot more dangerous.' He changed the subject abruptly. 'Old Know All here has been telling me that there's bit a of talk locally about Jane Bentley and this fellow Blane.'

Silver nodded. 'I was coming to that. Blane's a decent sort. I don't know what to make of it, Mr. Flagg, and that's a fact. Normally you wouldn't say much about it. If this hadn't happened nobody could have said anything about it. As it is, we'll have to have a word with him.'

'Then they are friendly?'

Silver shrugged. 'She comes around the hotel a lot. Gage says it's quite true. Miss Jane's been coming about four months now. She puts in a lot of her time with him —helping in the place—working on his books. Mind you, there may be no more to it than that, but Gage says it looks as if there is and he's not a man to exaggerate that sort of thing.'

'Does he think they're having an affair?'

'Most of the people in the community seem to think it. We'll have to walk carefully here, Mr. Flagg.'

'That's right,' Flagg said. 'Know All, you go along and

find this girl Edith you got all the gen from. Bring her in.'

Silver watched Newall go, frowning. 'I don't want to waste your time or mine on a red herring.'

'I'll take a chance on it,' Flagg said equably. 'Where's Blane now?'

'He went off to town this morning,'

The door opened as he spoke. Inspector Newall made his appearance, ushering in a slightly alarmed house-maid. 'Sit down, miss. This gentleman is Superintendent Flagg. He wants a word or two with you.' He looked over at Flagg. 'Miss Grove; Miss Edith Grove. Mr. Flagg would like to hear a bit about Mr. Blane and the Bentley girl, Edith. Just you take your time now. No hurry at all.'

She looked a little frightened. 'I hope I'm not going to get anybody into trouble.'

'I hope not,' Flagg said. 'But I don't expect you will. You know how it is, miss. We've got our job to do and that means asking questions. If it hadn't been for this murder cropping up, nobody would have bothered about what was going on—but when you have a thing like this everybody's got to do the best they can, haven't they? What sort of a boss is Mr. Blane?'

'A very nice gentleman, sir. He couldn't be nicer.'

Flagg raised one eye significantly. 'A bit fond of the girls, eh?'

She was quick to refute such a suggestion. 'Not Mr. Blane. He's a gentleman. No nonsense about him, let me tell you, and I knows what I'm talking about. I've been in places where you had to go around with a hat-pin in your hand. Good 'otels too—but a lot of gentle-men has funny ideas about maids. Some of 'em carry on like it was ancient Babylon that you read about in the Bible.'

'I'll bet they do,' Flagg said.

She nodded. 'Well, there isn't any of that kind of non-

100

sense here with Mr. Blane. That's what makes everybody so surprised about him and Miss Jane. She's such
a nice girl too—but it don't do at all to be shut up with
him there in his office for an hour or so at a time and
to be going for motor-car runs with him in the summer.
That's all very well—but people will talk.'

'You have to expect them to,' Flagg said sagely. 'They
do it every time. She spends her time in his room, does
she?'

Edith pondered. 'Not all of it—and maybe not even
very often. Not as much now as she used to at first. I
think Mr. Blane got to see everybody was noticing it.
But she goes there quite often yet. Does the books with
him and things like that.'

'Does Blane ever say anything about her being here so
much?'

'Not to me, he hasn't. He treats it like it was natural.
Maybe that's the best way. But he's bound to know
everybody's noticing it. That's about all I can tell you,
Inspector, and it's all anybody can tell you.'

'What about going away for motor-car runs?'

'That happens quite a lot. But I don't know where
they go.' She looked a little worried. 'I hope all this is
not going to get anyone into any trouble, Superintendent
—especially Mr. Blane.'

'I doubt it,' said Flagg. 'One thing more. What do the
people at the Close think of it?'

She shrugged. 'I can't tell you that, but they must
know about it.' She looked a little perturbed. 'These
things always get around and they'd find out somehow.'

Flagg said: 'You're very likely to be right there. Did
you ever hear of any trouble about it? I want you to
think this over carefully, miss. Did you ever have Mr.
Bentley down here?'

She swallowed. 'He was here yesterday.'

There was a little flicker of triumph in Flagg's eyes.
'Yesterday? Was he, now? You'd better tell us about it.'

'There isn't much to tell. He came along in the afternoon and went up to Mr. Blane's room. He was there for quite a little while, talking to him.'

'Tell us what you know about it.'

She did so, and they listened without comment or interruption. When she had finished, Flagg sighed. 'Well it's always something, miss. You can go back to your work. I wouldn't talk about this little interview if I were you.'

She rose, visibly relieved the interview was over. 'Don't you worry about that, sir. I don't want any trouble at all.'

'That's the idea,' Flagg said. 'You can let the young lady out, Inspector.'

Newall made his way over to the door, opened it for her, and nodded. 'There you go, Edith. We're much obliged for your help.'

She went out in silence, walked the length of the hallway, some apprehension in her heart. She had all but reached the stairway when she saw the tall figure standing in the shadows and halted. For a second she stared, then: 'It's you, sir. You give me quite a start there. I didn't see you till——'

Peter Blane looked at her grimly, then raised his finger authoritatively. He walked along the corridor towards his own room, reached it, and opened the door. He held it wide for her. 'Come inside.'

She stepped past him and the door closed softly.

17

For a long moment Blane stood there watching her, then, curtly, 'Sit down.'

She sat down nervously on the edge of the chair. 'Yes, Mr. Blane.'

He came over, standing with his back to the fire and looking down at her. 'You've had a little session with the police, Edith?'

The girl licked her lips. 'You saw me come out?'

'I saw you go in,' Blane said quietly. 'Now, my girl, I'd like to know what they had to say to you.'

'The superintendent told me not to mention it to anybody, sir.'

Blane laughed shortly. 'Maybe he did. But you're working for me, aren't you?'

'Yes. But I don't want to get into any bother.'

'You've got a fine job, nice food, good hours. Think it over, Edith. You've got quite a lot to lose. But you don't need to lose it. I'm not a vindictive man. They were asking about Miss Jane, weren't they?'

'Yes.' She looked a little shamefaced. 'And about you. I couldn't help that, Mr. Blane. I didn't tell them in the first place. They knew all about it.'

'I suppose they did. What did you tell them?'

She gave a brief account of her interview and Blane listened without apparent interest until she had finished. Then, he only nodded. 'Embarrassing for everybody, isn't it, Edith? It might have been just as well if you'd said nothing at all.'

'If it hadn't been me it would have been somebody else, Mr. Blane.'

He was willing to admit the truth of this. 'I suppose so. All right, Edith, you can go. And in future just remember this. You owe a certain loyalty to your employer. If people want to ask you questions about me, you'd better pass the word on. That way nobody gets annoyed. Do you understand me?'

'Yes, sir. But what if it's the police?'

'That goes for the police too.' He laughed softly. 'Very good, Edith. You may go now. No hard feelings either way. We'll say no more about it.' He walked over to the door then halted. For a second or two he stood there, then, 'So they're interested in me and Miss Bentley, are they?'

'They didn't say they were, sir. Just in the talk that goes on.'

'And what sort of talk goes on?'

'About you and her,' she said. 'Naturally, Mr. Blane, you don't expect me to tell you about it. It's just what you might imagine it would be.'

He laughed gently. 'I'll bet it is. All right, Edith.' He opened the door for her, held it until she had gone out. Then he went back and sat down in the big armchair beside the fire. For five minutes or so he sat there, then came to a decision. He left the room, walked stolidly down the hall until he came to the door of Superintendent Flagg's room. He knocked on the panel, heard a voice say, 'Come in.'

Peter Blane turned the handle and stepped inside. He said: 'Good afternoon, gentlemen. I'm sorry to interrupt. I heard Inspector Silver was here and I thought I'd come along. There's something that's been troubling me and——'

Superintendent Flagg looked suddenly interested. 'If there is, Mr. Blane, you've come to the right place.' He watched the hotel-keeper sit down. 'Now, Mr. Blane, if this is private business between you and the inspector here—just say the word.'

Blane shook his head. 'It isn't private. This is shocking news about poor Bentley. I can hardly believe yet that it's true.'

'It's true enough,' Flagg said. 'He was a friend of yours, was he?'

Peter Blane smiled without humour. 'I wouldn't exactly say he was a friend, Superintendent. I hadn't met him more than once or twice altogether.'

'But his daughter was a friend? Would you put it like that, Mr. Blane? Or would you put it stronger?'

Blane gave him glance for glance. 'I'd put it like that. Miss Bentley and I are good friends. Very good friends. I don't think you should get any wrong ideas about that.' There was a certain grimness in his tone. 'I can quite easily understand that there may be some speculation about our friendship. Under such circumstances there usually is.'

'And under such circumstances it's usually right,' Flagg said.

'Perhaps. It isn't in this case. But we're not talking about my friendship with Miss Bentley. We're talking about Bentley's death.'

'That's true,' Flagg agreed. 'And you came along to Mr. Silver about it.'

'Yes. The girl told me he was here.' Blane looked at Silver, then back to Flagg. There was some indecision in his eyes. 'Of course I haven't heard anything more about the murder, yet, than the news that came through in the morning, but I've had an idea all day I might have something for you.'

Silver looked interested. 'What's that, Mr. Blane?'

Blane leaned forward. 'I take it that you'll be checking up on most people in the neighbourhood, Inspector. You'll be interested in strangers and so on? Well, we had a man here yesterday who puzzled me. He came in in the morning and registered as John Warren of Cheam Road, Brockley.'

Silver looked suddenly interested. 'What about him?'

'He took a room,' Blane said. 'He thought he might be here for a couple of days or so. Now there's nothing

105

very strange in that, though we don't get many men who come here for a few days at this time of the year. Anyway, he didn't stay.'

'When did he leave?' Flagg asked abruptly.

'Last night. Round about ten-thirty. I wasn't here myself when he left. I'd gone into Reading. When I came back, Harker told me he'd come in, squared his bill and left. I didn't think very much about it till this morning and it's been on my mind ever since.'

Inspector Silver became instantly brisk. 'I should think so, Mr. Blane. We'll have some particulars about this Mr. Warren.'

Blane gave them methodically. 'Mark you, Inspector, I'm not trying to make trouble for the man. He may know no more about this than I do—but he was here at the time—and he disappeared pretty smartly. That's all I've got to say about it.'

'You didn't get the number of the car?'

'I didn't even see it. Harker says it was a Consul. I asked him about the number, but he had no idea. He wasn't even very sure about the colour. He thought it was green, but he couldn't be certain.'

'We'll have a word with him,' Flagg said.

Harker was produced, a stout, pleasant little man, and he corroborated most of Blane's information. The car was a Consul; in the night light it had looked green. He'd been busy at the time himself, tidying up the bar, and it was only because he'd gone out with a crate of empties to the store-room in the yard that he'd even seen the car at all.

They dismissed him, and Inspector Silver rose. 'I'll get through to the super, Mr. Flagg. I don't say this man Warren knows anything about it, but he'll have to be traced.'

'That's right,' said Flagg. 'Know All, you put through a call to Central Office and have Barratt handle it. Tell him to go out and get a statement from this man Warren.'

He tossed the butt of his cigar into the fire. 'Well, Mr. Blane, it looks as though you've given us something. That was what we were needing. Something to bite on.'

Silver and Newall made their way from the room. Flagg indicated them with a proper pride. 'You've put the forces of law and order into motion, as it were. Get the British policeman in action and you'll see something. Especially the younger ones like the inspector there and old Know All. Me—I'm too old and fat for all that kind of exertion. I've got to get my results in a quieter way. They tell me you had Bentley here to see you yesterday. What did he come up about?'

Peter Blane's eyes hardened. 'It was a personal matter.'

'I thought it might be,' Flagg said with satisfaction. 'But we've still got to look into it for all that. Was it so personal you couldn't talk about it?'

'It was,' Blane said shortly.

Flagg stroked at his cheek. 'That's a pity, Mr. Blane. When we don't know, we have to guess. That means we might guess wrong.'

'That would be your misfortune.'

Flagg smiled. 'It would be. It could be your misfortune too. We won't argue the toss. My guess is he came round to talk to you about his stepdaughter. He wanted you to do something about it—maybe to put a stop to it. Right or wrong?'

Blane rose briskly. 'I could lie to you, Flagg. I don't see why I should. Bentley came to see me just for that purpose.'

'Did you agree with him?'

'I did not.'

'I see,' Flagg said. He thought for a moment. 'You're fond of the young lady, Mr. Blane?'

'I'm very fond of her,' Peter Blane said.

'Did you quarrel with Bentley about her?'

Blane shook his head. 'No. We had no quarrel. I told him I couldn't see eye to eye with him.'

107

'While we're on the subject, Mr. Blane, what were you doing at the time Mark Bentley was murdered?'

Blane looked at him coldly. 'And at what time was that?'

'According to the evidence, between seven o'clock and eight o'clock last night,' Flagg said. 'Maybe nearer seven than eight.'

'I was on the way back from Reading at seven o'clock. I had a flat at Darisdale and I had to change a tyre.' He walked to the door. 'I'm afraid that's all I can tell you, Superintendent. Good afternoon.'

He went out, closing the door behind him. For a second or so he stood in thoughtful silence, then made his way along to his private room. Mark Bentley was dead. There were many reasons why he should have died a violent death. Peter Blane could think of one or two himself. For half an hour he sat there, then rose and crossed the room towards the desk. He was reaching for one of the drawers when he saw the envelope addressed to him, and he opened it and read the contents of the brief note.

The Trysting Tree at nine o'clock. He crumpled the sheet of paper and tossed it into the fire. It blazed up, and Peter Blane left the room to make his way downstairs. He went through to the kitchen and at the door met one of the girls.

'Miss Bentley was here sometime today, Linda. Will you find out if anyone saw her?'

The girl said: 'I saw her myself, sir. She left a note for you. Did you get it?'

'I got it,' Peter Blane said pleasantly. 'Yes, I got it.' He went back along the corridor a thoughtful man indeed.

18

INSPECTOR NEWALL returned to the room a few minutes later. 'Silver's gone,' he announced. 'We wanted to see Mr. Crayshaw. I got through to Barratt. He's going along at once to check up on Warren. I hope he can get hold of him right away.'

The big man chuckled. 'I don't know. I've got a feeling he may know something about it, but I doubt if he'll be easily found.'

Inspector Newall said bluntly: 'What about Blane? Where was he when Bentley got knocked?'

Flagg chuckled. 'According to my information he was on the road back from Reading. That's quite a good alibi to have. You can't say much about it and it's not very easy to disprove.'

'Who says he was on the road back from Reading?'

'Blane does,' Flagg said. 'Hand me over that manilla folder, Know All. We've got to go over this stuff as soon as we can. One thing you can say about these country policemen—they're thorough. They leave nothing out. You get hold of Russell and get back up to the Close. Have a word with Clancy and the young lady herself about how friendly she is with Blane. Pin her down as well as you can.'

Newall looked dubious. 'Do you think she'll tell me?'

'It's up to you to make her,' Flagg said significantly. 'It's a tricky job, I admit, but a man with all your education should be able to get to the bottom of anything. On your way.'

Inspector Newall left thoughtfully. Russell, he found in the kitchen behind the bar with a convivial pint in his hand, but in the interests of justice Russell was prepared to finish his pint with celerity and accompany him into the corridor, where he picked up his topcoat. 'Give me half a tick, Know All, and I'll be with you.'

Newall went out to the courtyard and here in the gathering dusk stood the police car. He was coming towards it when Russell appeared, slapping his heavy driving-glove sagainst his legs. 'Here we are. Inspector. The Close is it? What about Mr. Flagg?'

'He's got plenty to do to keep him busy here.'

Russell sighed. 'I well believe it. I'm glad I never got on any better than I did. This job suits me fine. I wouldn't change places with Superintendent Flagg for a five-pound note. There's nothing beats a good driving job, Know All. Take my tip and get on to the mobile side. Let other fellers have all the worry.'

'There's a lot in what you say,' Newall said moodily. 'You don't get paid for education in the Force. There's men, Russell, that are inspectors and chief inspectors and they couldn't tell you the difference between the atomic weights of tellurium and titanium. Ask 'em who was the first Plantagenet King of England and they wouldn't know what you were talking about. And if you got them on to Greek or Roman myths they wouldn't have a leg to stand on.'

Russell was in complete agreement. 'You never said a truer word. Look at old Dimm, an' him a chief inspector an' all. Here we are at the Lodge gates, Know All. There's a car coming down towards us on the drive.'

The lights ahead of them were dipped as they approached. The car swung past. Russell sighed. 'That's this feller Selwyn that's been at the Close.' He drove stolidly on to pull up in front of the big house.

Clancy came out to the door as they approached. 'Inspector Newall?' he said. 'Come in. Was there something special?'

'A talk,' Newall said. 'Is there some place quiet we can go, Clancy?'

Clancy led him to his pantry, and in the comfort of

this small and cheerful apartment Newall sank into a low, soft armchair. He looked round with some approval. 'Are we quite private here?'

'Nobody comes 'ere,' Clancy said positively. 'Mr. Mark maybe once or twice. Come in for a smoke or a pint if 'e felt like it. The women never come near.' He moved over significantly towards a cabinet. 'Would you care for a pint yourself, Inspector, or are you one of the kind of straight-laced cops that's never even 'eard of beer?'

Inspector Newall was quick to deny such narrow-mindedness. 'Not me, Clancy. I'll have a bottle any day and with any man.' He watched it drawn, then poured out into a wide-mouthed glass. Clancy passed it over.

'I usually 'as a mouthful about this time meself. Now then, Inspector, what's it all about?'

Newall looked over the brim of his glass. 'The young lady.'

'Miss Jane?' Clancy's thin face lengthened. 'What about 'er?'

'We've been hearing about her being friendly with the fellow at the hotel.'

'Blane?' Clancy scowled. 'Well, you know as much about it, Inspector, as I do. I've 'eard the stories. It's great 'ow people will talk.'

'It is,' Newall said. 'What do they say?'

Clancy looked at him suspiciously. 'I thought you said you knew?'

'I know what I heard.'

'I can't tell you anythin' about it, Inspector. As I live an' die, I can't. It's all 'earsay to me.'

'Did Bentley ever talk to you about it?'

Clancy looked irritable. 'Once or twice 'e mentioned it. I tried to keep 'im off the subject. In the end old Mark saw I was on her side, as it were, an' 'e stopped talkin' about it.'

'That's a pity. If you'd talked to him a bit more about it you might have had more information for the police.'

111

'Well, I didn't. That's all I can tell you.'

Newall drained his glass. 'If it is, it can't be helped. If it isn't, Clancy, I'll be back.' He rose briskly. 'Now I've got to see the young lady herself. Where do I go?'

Clancy got up. 'I'll go and see if I can find 'er, Inspector,' he suggested obligingly.

Newall cut him short. 'You can wait here, Clancy. I'll find her myself.' He went out into the hall, where he was fortunate enough to find a housemaid who was able to inform him that Miss Jane was in the morning-room.

'Tell her I'm here, miss. Name of Newall.'

Jane Bentley was sitting at one side of the fire when he went in, her eyes tired and wearied. There was strain in them, strain and something that might have been fear. Inspector Newall, who had seen it before, was not without some embarrassment. 'Well, miss, I'm afraid I've got to ask you one or two questions. I hope you don't mind.'

Jane said: 'No. Not at all, Inspector, if they'll help.'

'They ought to,' Newall said. 'But it's hard to say so early as this what's going to help and what's not. You can't hurry this sort of job, miss. You've got to take your time. Every now and then you get a little bit of new information that makes you wonder. Mr. Flagg wants to know one or two facts and you can help him better than anybody. How friendly are you with Mr. Blane?'

So suddenly did he put the question that a moment or two had slipped past before she realized the import of it. Then she felt the colour ebb from her cheeks. She stared at him, tense and frightened. 'With Mr. Blane?'

'The gent at the Knight Templar,' Newall explained pleasantly.

'I—I don't quite know what you mean.'

Newall sighed. 'Come now, miss. You know what these sort of places are like for gossip. Everybody's noticed it. Don't you try to make a mystery out of it. That'll only cause trouble all the way round.'

112

She had recovered herself. 'You've seen Mr. Blane, I suppose?'

'I haven't—but Mr. Flagg has. We've also seen two or three of the girls.' He looked at her sympathetically. 'Don't you get alarmed or upset, miss. We're not trying to make trouble for either you or Mr. Blane. But we've got to get to the bottom of these stories.'

She said quietly: 'I think I can see what you mean, Inspector. It's quite true that Mr. Blane and I are on friendly terms.'

'That's what we heard. How friendly?'

'Just very good friends. I can't say more than that. There's nothing wrong with spending your time with someone you like and admire, is there?'

Inspector Newall sighed. 'Who am I to judge, miss? What did Mr. Bentley think about it? I'd be glad to have your opinion on that.'

She coloured. 'He didn't say much about it at all. He only mentioned it to me once or twice altogether. Mark wasn't silly about a thing like that. He knew there was no harm in it. Why should there be?' She looked at him challengingly.

Inspector Newall shrugged his thin shoulders. 'There could be reasons, miss. But I'm not here to answer questions, my job is to ask them. Did Mr. Bentley ever tell you not to see Mr. Blane again?'

She gave him glance for glance. 'He never did.'

'Did he ever suggest you should stop seeing him?'

'Yes. And I told him I'd do as I pleased.' Her voice was calm. 'I'm not in the habit of letting people tell me what I've to do. Not even Mark.'

He looked at her with some admiration. 'And what did Mr. Bentley say to that, miss?'

She looked at him levelly. 'He dropped the subject.'

Inspecter Newall coughed. 'I'm afraid I won't drop it, miss. What did your mother think about it?'

The door opened as he spoke. He looked round over

one shoulder, saw the slim, youthful figure standing inside the room, and rose quickly.

Jane Bentley said: 'Here she is now. You'd better ask her. Mother, this is Inspector Newall of Scotland Yard.'

19

FAITH BENTLEY looked very pale and worn. She came across to where they were sitting, a querulous expression in her eyes. 'Who did you say the gentleman was, Jane?'

'Inspector Newall.'

'A policeman?' She sat down on one end of the sofa. 'I've been talking to them all afternoon, and I'm positively exhausted. Where's Johnny?'

'He went into the village,' Jane said. 'I think he wanted to see Inspector Silver. But you know Johnny and——'

'Johnny's been perfectly sweet,' the older woman said. 'It's very good of him to remain here with us. I can't get it into my head that poor Mark is really dead.' She looked at Newall without favour. 'Have the police found anything at all yet?'

Newall shook his head. 'A bit early yet, Mrs. Bentley. But we'll do the best we can.' He looked over at the girl. 'Well, miss, I don't think I need to wait any longer.'

'I don't think so,' she said calmly. She rang the bell at her hand. Clancy appeared a moment later, a little apprehensively.

'Is it me you want, miss?'

'Yes. Inspector Newall's leaving.'

Inspector Newall did so with dignity. 'Good night, Mrs. Bentley—and Miss Bentley. I'll maybe need to come

114

back again to go over one or two little points. You won't mind that?'

'No, Inspector.' She watched him leave, then went over towards the fire. Faith Bentley looked up at her curiously.

'What were you talking about when I came into the room, Jane?'

'About me,' the girl said quietly. 'Don't worry about it, Mother.'

'Goodness knows there's plenty to worry about,' the elder woman said. 'Jane, I wonder I don't go mad with it all. Poor Mark! It's so dreadful. It's going to be wretched with all these policemen around too—asking all sorts of questions. Really, you would imagine that at a time like this they'd respect your grief and your feelings. The things I've had to answer.' She shivered at the recollection of the hideous ordeal through which she had gone. 'Why can't they go about their unpleasant business quietly and leave people alone?'

'I suppose that would be too much to expect,' the girl said calmly. 'After all, they have their duty to do—and Mark was murdered.'

Faith shivered. 'But we don't know anything about that.'

'But the police don't know that, Mummy. They have to find out. Anyway, there isn't much point in talking like that. Even horrible and unpleasant things have to be seen in their proper perspective And now I'm going through to have Clancy set dinner for us. It'll be a lot nicer here together than in the dining-room.' She went through to the hall. The front door was still open so that a draught swept down the length of it. She heard it close as she stood there and in a moment Clancy came hurrying down towards her. He halted at the sight of her. 'Now, Miss Jane, what's all this?'

She said calmly, 'What was the inspector saying to you, Clancy?

He was vague. 'Nothin' in particular, miss. Just one

115

or two questions. Nothin' to get upset about. Just about him—Mark—and about me.'

'And about Mr. Blane and me?'

He closed his eyes in the excess of his emotion. 'As I live an' die, miss——'

'Don't lie to me, Clancy. I couldn't bear that.' There was a quality of pain in her voice which touched him.

'Well, I won't do that, Miss Jane. He was curious about you, but you know me. I don't hand out information to anyone—least of all about you.'

She smiled. 'Thank you, Clancy. And now let's be practical. Mummy and I are going to have dinner in the morning-room. You might set a table for us there. Mr. Selwyn will be back shortly, too.'

She went upstairs a little wearily, bathed her face and eyes. She was still in her room when she heard the sound of a car approaching and, in a moment more, the outside door open and close. When she went downstairs again, Johnny Selwyn was in the hall, puffing furiously at his large pipe. 'I wondered where you were, Jane. You look played out. Why don't you pack in and go to bed?'

'I wouldn't sleep if I did.'

'Take a tablet of some sort. The doctor gave some to Faith.'

'No thank you, Johnny. Anyway, I'll go after dinner.'

He looked pleased. 'That's the idea, Jane.' Then his voice altered. 'I saw the police arriving when I was going out. What did they want this time?'

'Information,' she said. 'Isn't that what they always want?'

'About what?' His voice was brusque. 'Why can't they leave you alone and get on with their own job. I'd like to give them a piece of my mind. When I was in the village I saw Flagg for a moment or so. They're at the Knight. I don't know why Blane takes them in at all.'

She laughed aloud. 'I'm afraid he couldn't refuse to take them.'

116

'I should,' he said venomously. 'Police are one class of people I've never had much patience with, Jane. I'd sooner have the burglars, or whatever they're there to hunt. Always sneaking around taking your number or asking for your licence. Always so damned important and pompous about things.'

'I didn't know you could be so vitriolic, Johnny.'

'I can be anything,' he said calmly, 'provided I'm angry enough. Let's go and have a drink. Clancy's late with dinner.'

'We're going to have it in the morning-room. Mummy's there now. She wanted to get up. We'd better go through to her.'

She led the way into the room. 'Here's Johnny, Mummy. He'll talk to you while I get some sherry.' She found a decanter and three glasses. Selwyn came across to carry the tray for her.

'I'm surprised to see you up, Faith.'

'I couldn't wait up there any longer,' Faith Bentley said. 'Not in that ghastly room with Dyer sitting looking at me and wanting to talk about it all the time.'

Johnny gave her a glass. 'Take this and forget Dyer,' he said sternly. 'That's what we've got to do. Get it out of our minds for a spell. And afterwards you'll get to bed and get some sleep—both of you. Do you more good than anything I can think of.' He looked round at them. 'That's my medicine. And here comes dinner.'

Clancy came in as he spoke. Dinner was an uncomfortable meal, for Faith Bentley was silent and tearful, and Johnny Selwyn's conversation and spurious gaiety so forced that the girl was grateful indeed when Clancy appeared with coffee.

A few moments later, Faith Bentley rose to go. 'Don't worry about me, Jane,' she said. 'Dyer is sleeping in my room tonight. You sit here with Johnny.'

Johnny shook his head. 'Not on your life, Faith. She's going to bed. The girl's washed out. You'd both better

117

get off now. I'll sit around for a spell. I don't expect we'll have any more visitors tonight, but you never can tell. Good night.'

They went upstairs together. It was almost a quarter to nine now and Jane was thankful for the insistence of Johnny Selwyn, which had made it possible for her to withdraw so easily. She found a stout pair of walking shoes, changed into a tweed skirt and jumper, then drew on a heavy coat. For a moment or so she listened by the doorway, but the corridor was silent. Cautiously she stepped out, making her way carefully to the servants' staircase at the rear of the house. A moment later she was on the gravel of the drive. There was a road which slanted up from the house, making its way on to the upper stretches of the moorland above. In a moment or so she had passed beyond the range of the house so that she was able to use a small pocket torch. She used it cautiously and walked along for some five minutes longer. Then, through the thinning plantation, she saw the sky and soon the black outline of a stone wall. She reached this and clambered over on to the narrow little road which lay beyond. Not more than a hundred yards away she could see the silhouette of the Trysting Tree. She had all but reached it, when she saw the black outline of the man who stood there. Peter Blane said softly: 'All right, Jane. I just beat you to it.'

He came out to meet her, put his strong arms round her. For a moment he stood like that, then he heard her sob. For minutes she sobbed, her head lying on his shoulder. He held her very tightly. 'Poor kid,' he said softly. 'Poor little Jane.' He leaned over and kissed her once. 'Try to forget about it, Jane. You can't keep on——'

She said wildly: 'Peter—you didn't do it, did you? You didn't kill him?'

His voice hardened. 'Pull yourself together, Jane. You've got to be more careful what you say. You never know who might be listening.'

118

She said: 'Nobody ever comes here. Nobody at all.'

He gripped her arm. 'Maybe not. But I don't propose to take any chances.' He walked her slowly down the road, and their voices died away softly in the distance.

A moment passed; the sound of their feet faded into the night, then a vast shadow detached itself from the grey bulk of the bushes by the roadside.

Superintendent Flagg sighed a weary sigh, changed his position and prepared to resume his vigil. It was well after ten o'clock by his large silver watch when he made his way back down to the main road. He had walked along it for close on half a mile before the lights of a car picked him out. It drew up beside him and a familiar voice said, 'I was beginnin' to think I'd missed you in the dark, Mr. Flagg.'

It was Russell. Flagg got in beside him stoically, sat back and stuck out his legs in front of him. 'All this excitement will be the death of me,' he said darkly, and for the rest of the drive he sat in brooding darkness. He left Russell in front of the Knight Templar, and pushed open the front door.

Peter Blane was standing by the fire talking to a customer. Now he came across solicitously. 'You're pretty wet, Superintendent. Been walking?'

'A bit,' Flagg growled. 'I shouldn't do it. Too old for it.'

Blane chuckled. 'If you'll leave your coat, Superintendent, I'll have it hung in the drying-room for you. I think the inspector's upstairs. Would you like something sent up?'

'Whisky,' Flagg said, 'and some hot water and lemon. Maybe a nip of sugar while you're at it.'

'I'll attend to it at once,' said Peter Blane, and for the next ten minutes he busied himself with this necessary work of mercy.

20

DAYLIGHT was just beginning to come into the sky next morning when Inspector Newall made his way down to the little dining-room, considerably surprised to find Superintendent Flagg already at the toast and marmalade stage. Newall came in and stood by the fire. 'Good morning, Mr. Flagg. I didn't hear you get up.'

'You didn't hear me get up,' Flagg said, 'because you were sleeping. You were sleeping, Know All, when other and more responsible parties were on the job.'

The girl came in with a steaming tray. Newall sat down. 'Where did you go last night, Mr. Flagg?'

'Out,' Flagg said, when she had gone. 'Blane went out. I thought I'd like to have an idea where he went. Russell and I followed him. We might have done worse. He met the Bentley girl. Up at the back of the house.' Flagg swore softly. 'The trouble was I couldn't get close enough to hear what was said. Well, we can't manage everything. You can get a move on, Know All. We're going to have a busy day.'

Inspector Newall looked up. 'What's going to happen?'

'We have a little talk with Clancy first,' Flagg said. 'That ought to clear the air a bit. We can do with it.'

He finished his tea, then made his way upstairs. Twenty minutes later, when Inspector Newall joined him, he was buttoning up his voluminous tweed coat against the rigours of early morning. 'What happens now, Mr. Flagg?'

'We get down to business. We'll get along now, Know All.' They made their way down by the main stairway. Peter Blane was standing in the hall with a pile of magazines in one hand. He turned as they came towards him.

'Good morning, gentlemen. I sent your coat up, Mr. Flagg, while you were at breakfast.'

120

Flagg stroked the sleeve of it. 'So I see. Dry as a bone and as warm as a pie. I checked your story about this fellow Warren, Mr. Blane. I had a report from London last night.'

Blane looked interested. 'What did they say?'

'They couldn't locate him. John Warrens there are in plenty, but there aren't any at 79 Cheam Road, Brockley.'

Blane looked puzzled. 'That was the address he wrote in the book. What do you mean to do about it, Superintendent?'

'Look for him,' Flagg said. 'He's important. It's a routine job and we can leave it to the Metropolitan Police. We'll get him all right.' He made his way out to where Russell was waiting in the big police car, the engine already running. On the way to Marchgate Close he was silent and Inspector Newall, who knew his reticent superior of old, was somewhat nettled.

'You've got an idea of some sort in your mind, Mr. Flagg?'

Flagg looked at him broodingly. 'Did you ever know me when I didn't have an idea in my mind? The trouble is, Know All, there are too many of them.'

'It doesn't look that way to me,' Newall said sceptically. They turned into the driveway and went up to the house. It was a housemaid who received them. Clancy, she thought, was in his pantry. She'd seen him but a few minutes before, and when they went along towards it, they found him standing in front of a small fire, and if he was surprised to see these representatives of the law at this early hour of the morning, he did not say so; instead: 'Well, gents, somethin' I can do for you?'

Flagg said: 'That's right, Clancy. You can begin by shutting the door.'

Clancy closed it, then came back. 'Sit down, Superintendent. I can't spend very long just now on account of the jobs I've to do. You got no idea about the amount of

121

work in a place like this, an' you can't trust the women.'

'There's a lot in that,' Flagg said. He sat down in the chair, patting his pockets as he did so. 'Now, here's a coincidence, Clancy. I've come out without a cigar again. It must be all the worry I've got on my mind.'

'I'll get one from the study,' the little man said. He moved to the door.

Flagg waved him back. 'The inspector here can go for them, Clancy. No bother at all. Know All, you just slip along to the study and bring the box back here with you. Now, Clancy, we'll get down to business.' And there was that in his voice which made the man stiffen.

'I'm sure I've told you all I know, Superintendent.'

Flagg looked at him balefully. 'And I'm just as sure you haven't, Clancy.'

Clancy looked harassed. 'If there's anything you've forgotten, all you've got to do is name it, an' I'll do the best I can.'

'You will indeed,' Flagg said. The door opened as he spoke and Inspector Newall came in, a large and ornate cabinet under his arm. Flagg nodded his approval. 'That's the stuff, Know All. Put it down there where we can see it.' He opened the lid and looked down at the long array of little silvered cylinders. 'It's a fine sight. We won't see many more like it in these days of high taxation and murderous prices. Well, it's up to us to do the best we can. What do you say, Clancy? Every man should put his shoulder to the wheel to help the government. I'll take one or two of these just in case.' He pushed them into his pocket, lit one, then rubbed his hands together. 'That's fine. I'm never at my best on a Sunday morning till I have a smoke after my breakfast. Now, Clancy, we'll get down to business. You and I and old Know All are going to have a bit a of a chat.'

Clancy licked his lips. 'I've told you all I can think of, Superintendent.'

Flagg sighed. 'Think harder, Clancy. Think hard

enough to take you back about twenty-four years. Can you manage that or do you need help?'

'It's a long long time,' the little man pleaded.

'Nark it,' Flagg said with sudden coarseness. 'I'm a busy man, Clancy. So much I can put up with and no more. Last night I had a message from Inspector Carmody of Fingerprints. You know what he was able to tell me? This will surprise you, Clancy. Old Carmody tells me you've done two stretches for larceny, nine months and a "two". What do you know about that, Clancy? You never brought the matter up.'

Clancy sat still staring straight ahead of him. 'I forgot about it.'

'Not you,' Flagg said. 'But you thought we'd forgotten about it. It just lets you see, Clancy. After twenty-four years the pigeons come home to roost. Do you want to talk about it—or do you want me to tell you?'

Clancy gave up the ghost. 'All right, Superintendent, I'll admit it. You can't blame me for not wantin' to bring it up. Let bygones be bygones. That's what I always say. Let these 'ere sleepin' dogs lie, that you 'ear all the talk about. And that had nothin' to do with Mr. Mark.'

'How do I know that, Clancy?'

'I'm tellin' you, ain't I?'

All the lethargy left Superintendent Flagg. He leaned forward briskly. 'You're telling me, Clancy—but that don't mean a thing. People are always telling me things and expecting me to believe them. All I know is you've got a record. Mark Bentley was murdered. The two things could hang together.'

Clancy drew in his breath. 'You don't think I knocked old Mark!'

Flagg sighed. 'I don't know yet who knocked him. I've got the idea you could help me a bit more than you've done. You can make up your mind, Clancy. Give me all the help you can—or take what's coming to you.'

The little man licked his lips. 'What do you mean?'

Flagg shrugged. 'I mean I'll turn in a report to the locals. They'll investigate you, Clancy. You've got a better idea than I have what they'll find out. Even if there isn't any more, it will still look interesting to them.'

There was a worried look in Clancy's eyes. For a moment he sat there in silence, then: 'All right. I'll tell you what I can. But it ain't much.'

'It never is,' Flagg said piously. 'We're thankful for small mercies, as the Good Book says. Get on with it.'

Clancy said: 'Like I say, it ain't much, but Mark had been gettin' 'phone calls that worried him recently. That was how it started.'

' 'Phone calls?'

'That's right,' Clancy said uneasily.

'What kind of calls were they?'

'Mark never told me what was said. All I know is it was a man's voice. There was three or four of 'em. Mark tried to find out who it was, but 'e didn't manage that.'

Flagg stared at him curiously. 'What did Bentley have to say about it?'

'After a while old Mark spoke to me about it. 'E told me it was somebody 'e used to know—but 'e never said who it was.'

'Did he know?'

'I don't think 'e knew. I think 'e guessed. But 'e never said to me 'e knew—or guessed. All I know is it was getting 'im down. Fair jumpy whenever the 'phone rang, 'e got.'

'When did these calls start?'

Clancy reflected. 'I first found out about 'em about ten days ago. I don't think it was long before that. But from then on we've 'ad 'em regular.'

'Did Bentley ever tell you what was said on the 'phone?'

'No. Not what was said. But whatever it was, it upset 'im.'

'He never said anything about threats—or blackmail?'

There was a little silence. Clancy shivered. 'No. Mark

124

never mentioned anything like that. But I'll tell you this, Superintendent, I did. It got me down pretty badly too —an' I asked Mark what the feller was after. But you couldn't get anything out of Mark if he was in that kind of mood. A day or so later 'e told me 'e was goin' to put a stop to it. He was goin' to get some private detective on the job.'

'And did he?' There was a certain keenness in Flagg's voice.

Clancy nodded. 'I 'eard 'im on the telephone, Mr. Flagg. A feller by the name of 'Udson. Lew 'Udson. Old Mark was makin' an appointment to see 'im. An' as I live an' die, that's all I know.'

'Lew Hudson,' Flagg said softly. 'What do you know?' He rose abruptly. 'I wish you'd told me this yesterday, Clancy.' He looked at the little man searchingly. 'That's all you can tell me? If you can think of anything else, Clancy, let's hear it now.'

'That's all,' Clancy said. There was the sound of a gong close at hand. 'That's for breakfast, Mr. Flagg. I got to go now an' get on with me work.' He opened the door, and drew up short.

Johnny Selwyn was standing with one hand on the handle.

'What's happening, Clancy? The whole household's sliding. Where's the porridge? Why is there no fire in the morning-room?' He looked over to where Superintendent Flagg stood. 'Flagg, you've disorganized the whole community.'

The superintendent sighed. 'Work—work, Mr. Selwyn. We never seem to get away from it. Did you know we were here?'

'Saw you arrive when I was shaving,' Johnny said with satisfaction. 'I wondered what was up. Even the constabulary don't go haring around the countryside at this hour of a Sabbath morning. Have you made an arrest?'

125

Flagg chuckled. 'Did you think we might have?' He went out into the hall. 'We'll get round to that in time enough. We usually do. Good morning, all.' He made his way briskly towards the door with Inspector Newall a lean and melancholy shadow at his back.

21

THE journey back to the Knight Templar was made in silence and it was not until they were turning into the courtyard of the hotel that Flagg gave them an indication of what was in his mind. 'We're heading back to London now,' he said. 'Give me a quarter of an hour to get a call through and some coffee.'

The coffee was brought to them in the lounge while Flagg was still absent and they sat down to it with unqualified approval. Russell lit his pipe and sat back in some comfort. 'It's a great thing too, Know All—all this rushing about of a Sunday morning. Back home the wife'll be getting the kids ready for the Sunday school. I'll miss that anyway. Normally I has to give 'em a word of comfort before they gets out.'

Inspector Newall was amused. 'I'll bet you do. I can remember what it was like when I was a bit of a nipper myself. Those were the days. The prizes I got for Bible knowledge were past all redemption. Enough books to fill a bookcase. It's an interesting thing the Bible. The first complete Bible to be printed in English came out in 1535. That was the one that Miles Coverdale brought out. The authorized version was published in 1611 as a result of the Hampton Court Conference in the reign of

James I. The longest and the shortest chapters in the Bible are both Psalms. I'll bet you didn't know that—Psalms 119 and 117 respectively, as the case may be. Quite a lot of verses in different books are alike. If you'll take the time to——'

The door opened and Superintendent Flagg came into the lounge. 'What's all this talk about Bibles and Psalms?'

'It's the inspector here,' Russell said. 'Old Know All's on about Bibles on account of its being Sunday.'

Flagg poured out some coffee for himself. 'Sunday's just like any other day when you're in the Force. I can remember fine when the girls were small, me getting out to the church once or twice.'

'Christenings?' said Inspector Newall knowledgeably.

Flagg looked at him suspiciously but there was no obvious evidence of insubordination here, or if there was Inspector Newall's lean features were singularly guileless. 'More than christenings,' he said darkly. 'But it's been a while now since I've got round to it. Usually on a Sunday morning I'm working. That's with being a superintendent. If I was a plain ordinary constable, like Russell here, the Branch Board would soon put a stop to that kind of nonsense.' He finished his coffee at a gulp. 'We'd better get on our way now.'

They went out to where the car waited. They drove for an hour or more in silence on roads on which the traffic was comparatively light, and it was not until they were within the Metropolitan area itself that Russell queried their destination.

Flagg was vague. 'Stop at the next telephone kiosk,' he said, 'and we'll find out.' He patted at his pockets. 'You got any change on you, Russell? I've got nothing but notes and we've got to put through an important call.'

'Not me,' Russell said frankly. 'I'm married, like yourself, Superintendent. Try old Know All there, that's rolling in cash.'

Inspector Newall seached his pockets without enthusiasm. He produced a handful of coppers and small silver coins, which were peremptorily commandeered.

'You remember just how much it is, Know All. You'll get it all back later,' Flagg advised. 'There's a kiosk ahead, Russell. Draw in here.'

The car was halted and he got out laboriously. In the kiosk, he dialled a number, then waited patiently. A moment passed, then a woman's voice said: 'Hullo. This is Mrs. Rapley speaking.'

'This is Superintendent Flagg. Is Inspector Rapley at home, please?'

'He's in bed,' she said. 'Having a long lie. Has he to go down to the office?'

Flagg chuckled. 'Hardly, Mrs. Rapley. This is a private business. I'm at a 'phone booth just round the corner. I want to see the inspector about something important. How would it be if I dropped round at the house?'

'Come round at once, Mr. Flagg.'

He thanked her and hung up. A moment later and he was back in the car.

'We're going round to Styles Place,' he said. 'Not three minutes' run, Russell. You cut round to the right and bear straight on.'

Russell, from a vast experience of police driving, was in no need of directions. 'I knows the place fine. An old inspector I once had lives round there at No. 97. Name of Rapley. A proper old bastard he is. What's the number, Mr. Flagg?'

'It's 97,' Flagg said. 'We're calling on my good friend Inspector Rapley.'

Russell was considerably surprised. 'Do you tell me that? I remember the old gentleman quite well. Very popular he was with the men.'

'I'll bet,' Flagg said significantly.

They drew up in front of a small detached bungalow and Flagg got out grumbling. 'They ought to make the doors of these things wider. Give me ten minutes or so. I won't be more than that.' He trudged up to the front door and rang the bell.

Mrs. Rapley led him through to a room with a fire in it. The inspector, it appeared, had not been exactly in bed after all. When Flagg had called he had been in the process of dressing, but this she had not known. 'He's shaving just now,' she said. 'He'll be through in a minute. One thing Dad can do smart is shave himself.'

'That's with being in the police,' said the knowledgeable Flagg. 'I'm the same myself. Two or three wipes with a razor and the job's done. All but drying the razor and the blade and the tidying up. I generally leave that to the wife. It keeps her from wearying now the family is grown up.'

Inspector Rapley came in a moment later, a large, potbellied old inspector with a fringe of grey hair, a bald head and a frosty-blue eye, which made him look as though he might be very highly respected at Divisional Headquarters. He came in, holding out his hand. 'Hullo, Flagg, I'm glad to see you. It must be all of three years since we met. I was sorry I didn't get you on the 'phone. I took a dose of salts this morning. Sunday's the only chance you get.'

Mrs. Rapley had discreetly withdrawn. Flagg looked at his colleague admiringly. 'You're looking fine, Rapley. I never saw you better.'

Inspector Rapley sat down, clearing his throat. 'If this wasn't Sunday morning and you weren't on duty——' he began.

Flagg held up his hand. 'Don't tempt me, Inspector. I've got a car load of mere constables and what not outside. I dropped round because I need a bit of help.'

Inspector Rapley looked interested. 'I'll do anything I can, Flagg. What's on your mind?'

'You've got a character in your district by the name of Hudson,' Flagg said. 'Lew Hudson—a private operator.'

Rapley looked interested. 'That's right, Flagg. He's got an office in Bailiff's Court. What has he been up to?'

'I don't know,' Flagg said. 'Not yet. I want a little talk with him. I'll give you the picture, Rapley, and you'll see what I mean.' He spoke for a moment or so, Inspector Rapley listening curiously.

'And now you want a word with him?'

'Right,' Flagg said. 'I don't know Hudson myself, but I know of him. As soon as I heard his name I said to myself: "Hudson is in Rapley's division. I'll get in touch with old Rap." My very words, Inspector, and here I am to prove it.'

Inspector Rapley considered. 'I know Lew Hudson as well as I know the back of my own hand. Used to be in the Force up in Manchester. He came here after the war and he's been in my division for six years now.'

'Is there anything against him?'

'Not yet,' Rapley said grudgingly. 'He's what you might call a border-line case. I've heard stories but there's nothing to back them up. He's clever, and he's done a bit of good work on commercial jobs—larcenies mostly. I've had my eye on him for a while. But there's been no complaints, mind you.'

'There's going to be one now,' Flagg said grimly. 'This Lew Hudson should have come forward and made a statement before this,' He looked at his watch. 'I wanted to have a word with you about him first though—just to hear what you thought. Now I'll take a run round to see him.'

Rapley blinked. 'Lives at Newsome Court,' he said. 'You wait till I get my boots on, Flagg, and I'll come round and introduce you.' He hurried from the room and there was the sound of a cupboard door opening and closing. In a minute or two he came back, buttoning himself into a wide raincoat. 'Here we are. It won't take too long. Did you say you had a car?'

They went out to it a moment later, and Russell greeted

130

his former superior with a sycophantic leer. 'Well, if it ain't Mr. Rapley! It's a long time since I've seen you, sir. Back in the old Stepney days. The first division I was in —and the finest. Happy days.'

Inspector Rapley was by no means impressed with these nostalgic remarks. He subjected Russell to a searching scrutiny, then nodded. 'I remember you. Russell—isn't it? There never was a man that caused me more trouble. On the carpet more than any other man I've met in my whole career.'

Russell sighed. 'Larking and joking,' he said defensively.

'Punting and boozing,' Inspector Rapley said reminiscently. 'I'm surprised to see you're still on the strength.' He settled himself down in the rear of the car. Flagg got in beside him.

'Here we are. The place we want is Newsome Court, Russell.'

He fumbled for a cigar, presented one to Inspector Rapley.

Rapley was considerably impressed. 'By jove, it's a whopper. Where did you get it?'

'On the case,' Flagg said. 'They supply them to me to keep me going. You say this fellow Hudson is smart?'

'Smart as you like.' Inspector Rapley mellowed slightly under the influence of a good cigar. 'We've never actually had anything against him, but you hear whispers. If even half of them are right—and I never believe any more than half—he can bear watching.'

'A one-man show, is it?'

'Practically. Once in a while he has to bring someone in for a shadowing job. When he does he sometimes gets old Tom Colling. You remember old Colling that used to be a sergeant at Wellington Arch?'

Flagg remembered Colling well. 'And he works for Hudson?'

131

'Occasionally. Colling's all right. He wouldn't do anything you or I wouldn't do. If you get stuck you might have a word with old Tom, though I don't think it would get you anywhere. If Hudson had anything fishy on his books, Colling wouldn't be likely to get a even smell of it.'

'It's worth bearing in mind,' Flagg said thoughtfully. 'What do you think he's been up to, anyway?'

Superintendent Flagg shrugged. 'That's what I'm curious about. I told you that Mark Bentley had employed him to do a little job for him. Why didn't he come forward when he heard Bentley was murdered?'

'Maybe he didn't hear about it,' Inspector Newall suggested.

Rapley sniffed. 'A character like this here Hudson gets to hear about everything, Inspector. Hearing things is his living.' He peered out at a line of fashionable flats. 'Here we are, Russell. Round the next corner—and along at the end of the block.'

They drove on slowly, swung round the corner. Rapley said: 'That's the one at the end there. No. 34 and one up.'

The car halted in front of No. 34. Flagg and Rapley got out. Newall pushed the door open, then looked around. He held the door open for them. 'Quite a smart-looking place, Mr. Flagg. This fellow Hudson must be in the right racket too. You don't do this on five hundred a year.'

There was a porter's box ahead of them, but of the man himself there was no sign. Inspector Rapley looked round him with the sternest disapproval. 'That's the way these places are run nowadays. No help when you need it. No consideration for the feelings of the authorities. We'll just go up.'

There was a little indicator on the stairway and from this they were able to discover that Lew Hudson occupied the right-hand flat on the first floor. They made their way up to it and the superintendent put his finger on the bell.

132

There was no answer. Again Flagg pressed the bell. They waited for a moment or two but the door did not open and Rapley was annoyed. 'I thought we'd have got him here,' he said disgustedly. 'It just lets you see the amount of bother some folk will put the police to, mind you. What do we do now? Do you want to try the office? It might be worth a tumble. If we don't get him there, I'm afraid we'll need to come back.'

Flagg did not answer. He leaned forward suddenly, pushing the flap of the letter-box inwards. Cautiously he peered through the slit, then looked up at them. 'Light's burning.'

Rapley scratched his head. 'What does that mean?'

Flagg straightened up. He crooked a finger at Inspector Newall. 'Put your nose to that, Newall, and tell me what you think.'

Newall bent over. He straightened up quickly.

'Cordite.'

'That's what I thought,' Flagg said. 'Rapley, it's your division. Should I kick the door off its hinges or go and look for the porter?'

Inspector Rapley breathed heavily. 'You think something's happened to him?' He raised his foot and stabbed heavily with his heel on the lock. The door swung open and Rapley pushed it wider. He went inside. There was a tiny hall which was in darkness, but in front of them a door stood wide open. There was a light in the room, and it was this light Flagg had seen.

Now the Central Office man went forward sniffing the air. 'That's cordite all right.' He pushed open a door and stood still. There was a man in pyjamas and dressing-gown lying on the floor in front of them, his head against an armchair.

Rapley licked his lips. 'Lew Hudson,' he said. 'That's him.'

'Dead,' Flagg said. 'Just like Mark Bentley.'

133

22

SUPERINTENDENT FLAGG got down on his knees. He examined the dead man briefly. 'He was shot at close range. My guess is he was sitting on that chair. He started to get to his feet and he was shot.'

Newall went round him and subjected the chair to a searching scrutiny. 'There's a long jagged rip here, Mr. Flagg. It could be the bullet. It may have ended up in the chair. I can't see where it left it.'

Flagg said: 'Inspector, you'd better get through to D.H.Q. It looks like I've really spoiled your Sunday for you.'

Rapley sighed. 'If it wasn't this it would be something else. Imagine a killing right on my own doorstep like that. The bloody impertinence of it.' He went out of the flat and they heard him close the door. He was back in a matter of moments. 'That's that. The boys will be over from D.H.Q. in a minute or two. I put in a call from the flat next door. A character name of Maley. He thinks he heard the shot. It was about ten minutes to ten o'clock this morning.'

'This morning? That's a help. Get him in.'

Maley was brought in a few moments later. He was a pleasant little man in his mid-sixties and considerably perturbed by the proximity of violent death. 'Imagine poor Hudson going out like that!' he said. 'Such a quiet man too. You hardly ever saw him around at all.'

Flagg showed him a chair. 'Yes, Mr. Maley. It's a nasty proposition. Well, we'll have to get after the killer as soon as we can. Mr. Rapley said you heard a shot. We want to know all we can about that.'

Maley was positive enough about the sound he had heard, and about the time. His manservant had had the week-end off and Mr. Maley had had to rise to make his early-morning tea. He had done so and had gone back to bed at exactly five minutes to ten. He had just been in bed for a moment or so when he heard the sound. He had been lying there wondering what had caused it when he heard ten o'clock chiming on his mantel clock.

Flagg listened carefully. 'What did you think the sound was?'

Maley shook his head. 'I couldn't think what it was at all. It puzzled me—on a Sunday morning. I knew it wasn't a backfire, and I wondered if it was maybe something that had fallen, like a book—but it didn't sound like that either. I lay for a while listening but nothing happened and nobody was moving around, so I didn't think any more about it.'

'How loud was the sound?'

Maley frowned. 'Not very loud at all. Not like a pistol shot. It wasn't a crack or anything like that. If it hadn't happened just through the wall from me, and on a Sunday morning when everything was quiet, I don't expect I'd have heard it.'

'I don't suppose you would,' Flagg said. He questioned the man further. He had not heard anyone going up to the flat, but he had heard Hudson's telephone ring some time earlier. He could not be sure at what time it had been, but he thought it had probably been the telephone which had wakened him first of all.

Flagg dismissed him, handing him over to the men from D.H.Q., and went through to where Lew Hudson was still lying on the floor of the sitting-room, and noticed what he had not noticed before. An electric radiator at one side of the chair had been switched on. He indicated it to a detective. 'Did you switch this heater on, officer?'

The man shook his head. 'No, sir. The heater was on when we arrived.' Flagg went across and sat down, and in a moment or so Inspector Newall came.

'What a caper, Mr. Flagg. Here we come all this way to see Hudson and this has to happen. What do you think?'

'I know what I would like to think,' Flagg said darkly.

Inspector Rapley looked into the room. 'Here you are, Flagg. I've been having a word with the doctor. He agrees that Hudson was probably shot round about ten o'clock this morning. It looks like Maley was right. Did you hear about the telephone ringing in Hudson's flat earlier in the morning?'

'I did. I'm interested in that.'

'Ten past nine,' Rapley said. 'The lady above heard it too. She puts it at that time—and it's close enough to Maley's own time to be true.'

'She didn't hear the shot?'

'No, but she was running a bath for herself a few minutes before ten o'clock. She couldn't be expected to hear anything. What a job! I've had a word with the porter. He can't tell me a damn thing. Feller by the name of Wheeler. He has a basement flat, but he doesn't come on duty till one o'clock on a Sunday. He neither saw nor heard anybody. That's the biggest pity of all.'

'It is indeed,' Flagg said. 'It was a pity Hudson had to get knocked. Well, it just lets you see what can happen when you poke your nose into what doesn't concern you.'

'Who killed him?'

Superintendent Flagg sighed. 'I wish I could tell you that. But I'll tell you why he was killed. He was killed because he'd done a little job for Mark Bentley.'

Rapley looked startled. 'You think the two killings are tied up together?'

'I'll be surprised if they're not,' Flagg said. 'Now we'd better get a move on, Inspector. The first place we make for is Hudson's office.'

Rapley nodded. 'I've thought of that. There may be something there. He doesn't keep any correspondence on

136

file at home.' There was a stern disapproval in his voice. 'That's a bad mistake. In case of emergency there always ought to be something around to help the police.' He looked over at Flagg. 'Say when you're ready, Superintendent.'

'I'm ready now,' Flagg said. 'The sooner we get over to Hudson's office the better pleased I'm going to be.' He made his way towards the door. They went down to the car where Russell received them with some curiosity, tinged with a vague disappointment.

'What's all this about somebody getting knocked, Mr. Flagg? I heard the rumour from the man at the door. It gave me an awful fright. I thought maybe it was Inspector Rapley here, but I see he's safe and sound.'

Rapley got into the back of the car, sniffing suspiciously. 'An awful smell of smoke so far as I can see,' he observed darkly. 'We're going round to Bailiff's Court, driver.'

They drew away. On the road, the divisional inspector put forward his own point of view. 'It looks as if the murderer was somebody Hudson knew quite well, Superintendent. From what we hear, he may have 'phoned Hudson and told him he was coming over. Hudson must have let him in. He got up and put on a dressing-gown and went to the door. Then they sat down to talk. Hudson switched on that radiator. That all looks as if they knew each other well enough.'

Flagg was in complete agreement. 'I think you're right.'

Rapley said: 'Well, we'll get him. Maybe it'll take time—but we'll find somebody out who saw him go up to the house. In broad daylight too. Ten o'clock in the morning. Imagine starting off the day like that an' it a Sunday too.' The enormity of this offence seemed to rankle deeply. 'Have you got any ideas?'

Flagg chuckled. 'I've got ideas,' he said cautiously. 'But you know me, Rapley. I never open my mouth till I know where we stand. The only thing I'm sure of

137

is that Hudson's death is connected with the Bentley murder.'

'I hope you're right.' said Inspector Rapley. 'If you are, you'll get this one handed to you on a plate. I could do fine without it. I don't like murders in my division. There's plenty of bother without the like of them.' He peered around him with a certain fixity of purpose. 'Here we are, Russell. This is No. 11. Stop at the second doorway there.'

The car drew up. Flagg made for the stairway, Inspector Newall close behind him. They made their way up to the second floor with Rapley puffing behind them. There was a door ahead of them, and on it in black lettering:

GARNETT AND HUDSON
Private Investigators

Superintendent Flagg tried the handle. It was locked. He looked round at Rapley. 'We'd better break it open, Inspector.'

Together they forced the door open and went into the outer office. Rapley pointed to the communicating door. 'That's Hudson's room in there. Did all his work in it.'

The door was unlocked. Inspector Newall pushed it open then stepped inside. 'Someone's been here.'

This was undeniably true. Ahead of them stood a tall metal filing cabinet. One of the drawers stood open. There were one or two cards strewn on the floor as though they had been examined hastily and as hastily discarded. The drawer of the desk was open, though there was no evidence that its contents had been disturbed. Flagg went over towards the filing cabinet, stooped down to lift a card from the floor. It was a plain white card; on one side, written in a rather large and legible hand, were a few words and these he read aloud:

138

'Employed by Sedley and Sanderson. Age 41. Married. Lives at 12 Lynane Ave, Hampstead:

AVERY, PETER, WILSON.'

He dropped the card to the floor and inspected the drawer. On the green metal door of the drawer was the designation: A—D.

He looked around to where Inspector Rapley stood. 'It looks like we're too late, Inspector. Now we'll do what we should have done in the first place. I must be getting old or something. I'm slipping badly.' He turned back towards the door.

Inspector Rapley looked a little puzzled. 'What do we do now?'

Flagg made for the doorway. 'Find Tom Colling,' he said. 'Before somebody else finds him.'

23

EX-SERGEANT COLLING they found in Acton, a large, burly old man who received them with considerable surprise. He showed them into a small sitting-room, apologizing as he did so for the lack of a fire. 'We never puts it on till after we have our dinner, gentlemen. What can I do for you?'

Flagg said: 'I'm hoping you can do quite a lot, Tom. We've got a murder on our hands. Lew Hudson.'

Colling pushed his fingers inside the neck of his rather tight collar. 'Lew Hudson! That's a caper for you. I can hardly believe it. When did it happen?'

'This morning about ten o'clock.' Flagg gave him a

brief account of what they had learned. 'The inspector here tells me you've done a bit of work for him, so we came around to see if there was anything you could tell us.'

It was evident that Sergeant Colling considered the situation came under the category of a crisis and as such merited especial treatment. He opened a cupboard, then produced a tall green bottle and four glasses. 'First of all we'll have a little drink. This has upset me, gents. Poor old Lew.' He poured out whisky with a steady hand and gave them each a glass. Then, when he was settled: 'Now what is it you want to know?'

'As much as you can tell us about him.'

The old man shook his head. 'That won't be a great deal. Hudson was a pretty reticent kind of feller. I've worked on and off for a couple of years for him but I still don't know anything about him or his affairs. That was the kind of man he was.'

'He didn't take you into his confidence?'

'He did not. He was a quiet sort of feller. Any more than telling you what the job was, an' to get on with it, he never opened up at all.'

'Did you do much work for him?'

Colling considered. 'Quite a lot. He ran a one-man business and I think he made quite a good thing out of it. But he handled everything himself. Most of the work was confidential.'

'Did anybody else work for him?'

Colling frowned. 'I don't think so. I used to wonder about that. Before he took me on he had old Sandy Cameron. But Cameron's wife died two or three years ago and Sandy went up to Scotland to live with a daughter. I've never heard of anybody else doing anything for him.'

'What sort of fellow was he to work for?'

'Lew was all right. He gave you your instructions and let you get on with it. He never interfered at all. I turned in a report to him every day I was on a job. He was kind of fussy about that—methodical, you might say. He figured I knew my job and he let me get on with it. He was quite a good feller to work for.'

Flagg said softly: 'Tell me this, Tom. Was he on the hook?'

Colling scratched at a large hairy ear. 'Damned if I know, Superintendent. He did quite well out of it, I can tell you that. He had a nice big Jaguar car and a bit of a cottage at Marlow—and this here flat in Newsome Court. I never saw anything that made me feel he was on the hook. But he could have had one or two lines with good pickings for all I know.'

'Such as what?'

'Blackmail. That's the first thing you think about with a private operator. Most of these boys get to hear a lot about what's going on. They can't help finding out. That's their business. And if they find out something important enough, about somebody big enough, it could be a good seam for the rest of their lives.'

'You never said a truer word,' Rapley said. 'Many a time I've seen it and——'

Flagg leaned over. 'But you haven't got any suspicions about Hudson?'

Colling had not. 'No suspicions at all. Like I say, I've wondered—but I've got nothing to back it up at all. Only the sort of ideas you get. What's it all about, Mr. Flagg? Why was Hudson knocked? What was the idea?'

Flagg sighed. 'Did you ever hear Lew Hudson mention a client of his by the name of Bentley? Mark Bentley?'

There was a little glint in Colling's eyes. 'Bentley? He was the feller that was murdered somewhere in Berkshire the other day? Mr. Hudson never mentioned him to me.'

Flagg said: 'That's a pity. Bentley consulted him the day before he was killed. I'd like to know why.'

'You're sure of that?'

'I'm sure of it. Bentley's manservant told me about it.

I think he was right. What was the last job you did for Lew Hudson?'

Colling started. 'It had nothing to do with anybody called Bentley.' But there was an odd look in his rather faded eyes. 'It's queer you should ask, because this one puzzled me a bit. Hudson didn't touch divorce jobs. Most of the private men need them to live—but he stood clear of them. But this last job I've been on had all the earmarks of one.'

Flagg rubbed his big hands together. 'A divorce job? Do you tell me that, Colling? Let me know all the details. Nothing too bad, I hope?'

'I did a bit of work on it for a week or so,' Colling said. 'All there was to it was keeping an eye on a woman that lived in Marley Lane. 24 Marley Lane. Hudson said he'd heard she was going about with somebody or other and he wanted to get the facts on it. She was a Mrs. Eve Bolton. She was a kind of blowsy blonde that had seen better days. I hung around and had a word or two with the neighbours an' kept my eyes open. It was true enough. They'd seen him about quite a bit. Once or twice they'd gone out in a cab together.'

'You ever see him, Tom?'

'Twice. He looked to be about my own age—maybe about five feet ten or so. A strongly built man. He walked with a bit of a limp. But I didn't get very close to him. Hudson told me to keep my eyes open but not to be seen on the job. I didn't take any chances and I got most of my information about him from a feller who lived in the next flat to Mrs. Bolton—a feller called Sandford. This Sandford was a manservant to a gentleman that was abroad an' he was keeping the flat open. He had a lot of time on his hands and he was quite interested in Mrs. Bolton himself.'

'Well, well,' Superintendent Flagg said pleasantly. 'And that was all there was to it? Nothing interesting, eh, Tom?'

142

'Nothing at all,' Colling said. 'That was what puzzled me. I couldn't think why he was interested in it. It wasn't his line of work. But I did what I was told an' I turned in a report on this here Varney——'

'Varney?'

'That was his name. Sandford got that out of Mrs. Bolton. Sid Varney. But he didn't talk about him much. My own opinion is this Varney was blind or something. She looked like hell an' she drank like a fish. Sandford said the gin bottles they carry out of there at the weekend is a disgrace. That's all I can tell you about that, Mr. Flagg. It isn't very much, but you'll find a report I turned in on it in Hudson's files. You take a look through those files and you'll maybe get somethin' else.'

'The files are gone,' Flagg said.

Colling started. 'What do you mean? Gone where?'

'I wish I knew. We were over at Bailiff's Court before we came here. Someone broke into the office and lifted cards from the A—D files.' Flagg laughed harshly. 'That covers both Bentley and Bolton. I don't think we'll have much luck there. But maybe you've given us more than you knew, Tom.'

Sergeant Colling shook his head. 'I never knew the like. Lew Hudson gets knocked and his files broken into. You want to have a look at her, Mr. Flagg. That'll put you right.'

'It's a good idea,' Flagg said. 'Mrs. Eve Bolton, 24 Marley Lane, Chelsea. Maybe it wouldn't do any harm to drop over and have a look at her. Or a word with her,' he added significantly.

Inspector Rapley was in complete agreement. 'I don't understand a damn word of it,' he said pleasantly, 'but you've got to begin somewhere. Anyway I'll be quite glad if you do, Flagg. It gets you out of my division, an' the sooner you get out the better, before somethin' worse happens.'

Superintendent Flagg chuckled. 'There's something in

what you say, Rapley.' He rose as he spoke. 'Well, Tom, you've maybe given us something worth while. In a case like this everything helps.' He thanked the old man and they went out to where the car was waiting for them. 'What about you, Inspector? Where do we drop you now?'

Inspector Rapley was prepared to settle for Divisional Headquarters. 'If I don't turn up there, they'll be sending out to look for me,' he said, and towards this lowering edifice they made their way. He took his leave of them in front of the building. 'I'll let you know as soon as we have anything on this Hudson job,' he said. 'We'll turn up something, Flagg. I hope you can use it. You're going to handle this business about Mrs. Bolton?'

'Right away,' Flagg said. 'I'll give you a ring if anything comes out of it.'

'I doubt it.' Rapley raised a hand in salute. 'On your way, Russell. Watch your corners. You're taking them wide—wide. You can get away with that sort of drivin' in some places—but not in my division.'

They drew away. Inspector Newall said admiringly: 'Listen to the old perisher, would you? An old battle-axe.'

'An old bastard,' Russell said. 'What did I tell you! That kind never change. Did you say Marley Lane, Mr. Flagg?'

'Marley Lane,' Flagg agreed, and sat back in speculative silence for the duration of the journey.

24

MARLEY LANE was a short street composed of tall red-brick houses, and No. 24 was the last of a block of six. They drew up in front of it and Inspector Newall led the way upstairs. He halted in front of a door at the end of a hall on which a white card rested in a metal slot. On it was printed:

MRS. EVE BOLTON

'This is it,' Newall said. He touched the bell and together they listened to it ring farther back in the flat. There was the sound of a dog barking. The barking became louder, and a woman's voice said:

'Quiet, Chang. Quiet, darling.'

The door opened. They saw a woman in her late forties, large, fair, her ample figure swathed in a scarlet silk kimono. There were two Pekinese snuffling at her heels, and with the opening of the door they began to bark again. 'Be quiet, pets! Don't be tiresome!' She looked up almost irritably. 'What is it?'

Inspector Newall introduced himself bluntly. 'Police, ma'am. Name of Newall. Inspector Newall of Central Office. This gentleman here is Superintendent Flagg. He wants to have a word with you.'

She looked at them with a sudden curiosity. 'Police? What do you want with me? I don't know anything about——'

'We'll go into that inside,' Flagg said breezily. 'We've got quite a lot to say, Mrs. Bolton, and of course we don't want to have to do it on the doorstep. You never know who's listening.'

She looked at him sharply. 'That's true enough. Come in. Don't mind the dogs. I don't get many visitors and the little darlings get so excited.' She led them through to a large, untidy room. A large electric radiator was glowing a little to one side of it, and an armchair had been drawn up in front of this. There was a small table at hand, on which Flagg saw an open box of chocolates, a cigarette box, a wineglass with a smear of lipstick on it and a little gin still at the bottom of it. He sat down without invitation.

Eve Bolton sat down herself. There was a fair smell of gin in the air, superimposed on the odour of burning milk, and of this latter she was obviously conscious. She sniffed dismayingly. 'I hope the smell doesn't annoy you. I was making a meal for the dogs and the damn milk boiled over. You just can't be every place at once, can you?' She looked over at Flagg. 'Now, Mister— what did you say your name was?'

'Flagg. Superintendent Flagg of Central Office,' he said woodenly. 'And you are Mrs. Eve Bolton?'

'That's right. What's all this about? What is it you want? I hope the neighbours haven't been complaining about the dogs again. You would think they'd be a little kinder. They talk about the English being animal lovers, but——'

Flagg sat back heavily. 'What about Mr. Bolton? Where is he?'

Her eyes suddenly hardened. 'My husband is dead.'

'That's a pity,' Flagg said. 'When did it happen?'

'Years ago,' she said. 'I wasn't married very long at the time.'

Flagg looked appropriately distressed. 'You'll have his death certificate handy I expect, Mrs. Bolton. I'd like to have a look at it—along with one or two other things—all in the line of business as it were.'

She stiffened. 'What sort of things?'

'We'll go into that later, Mrs. Bolton. Right now if you'll get the certificate I'll have a look at it. It's important and——'

146

She shook her head. 'I'm afraid I haven't got a certificate, Superintendent.'

Flagg looked considerably astonished. 'Why is that, Mrs. Bolton?'

'Bert was killed in the war,' she said. 'Out East—I got a letter to say he was expecting to go to Malaya soon and a week or two after that Singapore fell. I've always thought he was lost there. Nobody ever heard from him again. I certainly never did. That's about all I can tell you.'

'Was he in the army?'

'He was in the Merchant Service. On a Greek line. I couldn't even give you the name of the boat now. Sixteen years is a long time.'

'It is,' Flagg said. 'You would be quite a nice-looking woman in those days. Thirty-one or so—no more than that.'

'What do you mean?' There was a startling venom in her voice. 'Thirty-one? I was only a kid then. Just a girl —and a damned foolish one at that.' Her flash of temper left her as suddenly as it had arrived. 'I'm sorry if I was rude, Superintendent. A man of your experience should know better than to twit a woman about her age. But I've always been touchy about Bert. It was a mistake to marry him—if I'd been older it wouldn't have happened.'

'You mean it wasn't a happy marriage?'

She shrugged. 'What do you expect? I was just a kid —and the war was on. He was pretty fond of a good time himself. I never saw him much after we got married. Just for a few days—and then he went away.'

'And he never came back?'

'No. I tried to make some inquiries about him after the war was over. But the Company had closed down during the war. Their records were lost. They couldn't give me any information about him at all.'

'So you gave up trying to find out?'

'That's right. Do you blame me? If he was alive it

147

was up to him to do something too. He could have come back—but he didn't. Anyway, you need money to make those kind of inquiries. I never had any.'

'I see,' Flagg said. He took a look of honest appraisal around him. 'You look like you're fairly well fixed here.'

'I'm comfortably off,' she said. The wary look was back in her eyes. 'But what's all this about, Mr. Flagg? I don't understand why you're——'

'You'll understand soon,' Flagg said. 'What do you think, Inspector?'

'You took the very words out of my mouth,' Newall said. 'You've got a fine place here, Mrs. Bolton. Enough ornaments to stock a china shop. Pictures too. Some of them are as fine as anything I've seen for a long time. That one there—"The Sword of Damocles"—is as fine a thing as I've come across.'

Flagg looked across at it. 'So it is. A man having his tea. But where's the sword all the talk's about? That's what I want to know.'

'Look above him, Mr. Flagg,' Newall said significantly. 'There you go. This Damocles was a great fellow for flattering and soft-soaping people. They made him sit at a feast with that sword you see there hanging by a single horse hair, right over his head. Enough to put anybody off his meal.'

'I should think it would be,' Flagg said forcibly.

Eve Bolton looked interested. 'I didn't know about that. Is it true?'

Inspector Newall smiled a weary smile. 'Is it true? Would I be sitting here telling you a lie about it, Mrs. Bolton? I ask you. It's a well-known fact of Greek history or mythology as the case may be. I'm a student of it.'

She was impressed. 'I didn't think that kind of thing would interest a policeman very much. History and stuff like that.'

He smiled a quiet smile of polite amusement. 'There's more than one kind of policeman, Mrs. Bolton. There's

148

the ordinary common kind that's more interested in punting, and football pools and beer. Then there's the other kind like me that spends the time picking up culture. History is my speciality. I could tell you things about it that would open your eyes. When was the battle of Thermopylae fought? That was the one where the Persians defeated the Greeks. Easy. It was 480 B.C. When did Alexander the Great become King of Macedonia? So far as I'm led to believe it was in 336 B.C. Not many people could tell you that. I'm one of the few. But history isn't everything. There's literature, mathematics. Take science.

'What's the pressure of the atmosphere? It's fifteen pounds per square inch, but how many people could tell you that? The light of the sun takes about eight minutes to reach the earth. What about icebergs? In a normal season in the Atlantic you don't get many more than about 320. That's quite enough—and while we're on the subject— only about one tenth of the iceberg can be seen above the water. Some people say a third—but I doubt it. That brings us to the number of muscles in the human body—and here's an interesting fact. You can't——'

Flagg said, 'While we're on the subject of interesting facts—here's an interesting question.' He looked at the woman as he spoke. 'Have you ever heard of a man called Mark Bentley?'

If he had expected her to show surprise he was disappointed. Eve Bolton looked at him without interest. 'Mark Bentley? Who is he?'

'He's dead,' Flagg said. 'Like Bert Bolton.'

She glanced over at him. 'Is that supposed to be a crack, Superintendent? If it is you can skip it. I don't like those kind of gags.'

Superintendent Flagg smiled a nasty smile. 'You've never heard of Bentley?'

'No. What did he do?'

'He got murdered.'

149

There was a little silence. Her mouth sagged open. For one second she stared at him, then: 'Murdered? No, I've never heard of him. What makes you think I might?'

'I wondered,' Flagg said. 'I'm investigating the case. We've found out quite a bit about Mark. Ever met a character by the name of Hudson?—Lew Hudson?'

'Lew Hudson? No, I've never met him. What is this?'

'There's an awful lot of folk you've never met,' Flagg said unpleasantly. 'The police never get much help at any time. Well, I'm wanting a bit of information about somebody you have met. What about Sid Varney?'

There was a little silence. Eve Bolton stared at him. Then the colour left her cheeks. She gave a little sigh, then slid to the heavily carpeted floor in a large and fleshy heap.

25

SUPERINTENDENT FLAGG could move with celerity when speed was demanded. Now he bent over the fainting woman and, lifting her, carried her over to the long sofa on which a cat and one of the dogs lay, watching him balefully.

'Get those damned articles off of there, Know All.'

Newall swept them off with a bony arm. He went over to a decanter, removed the stopper and sniffed. 'Gin. That'll have to do, though I wouldn't give it to the animals myself.' He poured some into a glass.

Flagg held it to her lips. 'Here you are, Mrs. Bolton. Drink it up.'

Her eyes were open now, but her fleshy features were

grey. Then, after a moment, she took the glass into her own hand. 'Thank you, Superintendent. What happened? Did I faint?' She looked at him almost coquettishly. 'It's a long time since that happened. I used to faint a lot at one time though. One doctor said my heart wasn't too good. It's all this talking and asking questions. It's thinking about Bert again after all these years.'

Flagg was not impressed by such a theory. 'It was thinking about Varney,' he corrected. 'Sid Varney. Now, you take a rest for a minute or two, Mrs. Bolton, and after that we can finish our little talk.'

She had pulled herself together again. Now she laughed, a grating little laugh. 'If it's Mr. Varney you're interested in, you'll get nothing from me, Superintendent. He's a friend of mine. I'll go the length of saying quite a good friend. But you don't talk about your friends. Not if you've been brought up like me. Not that I could say anything about him anyway. I hardly know the man.'

For a second or so she pondered this remarkable statement, then its inconsistency seemed to become apparent to her. 'What I mean is, I haven't known him for very long. He's quite a gentleman anyway.'

'I'll bet he is,' Flagg said admiringly. 'Did he help out with any of this, Mrs. Bolton?'

She looked at him coldly. 'No, he didn't. And you've got no right to talk to me like that. Such a suggestion. I'm a decent woman and——'

Flagg sighed. 'I'll bet you are, Mrs. Bolton. As decent as the next one. And now we'll have some plain speaking. You've got yourself mixed up in a killing. You know what happens to people who do that.'

She shivered. 'But I don't know——!'

Flagg held up his hand. 'You'll know in a minute or two. I'm investigating the murder of Mark Bentley. You didn't know him?'

'I told you I didn't,' she said sullenly.

151

'You can tell me anything,' Flagg said grimly. 'All right. We'll come back to that. You've mixed yourself up in something, Mrs. Bolton. I don't say you know any more than you say you do. If you don't, you've got no worries at all. I wish I had as few. But you've got to be investigated. You've got to help us all you can. You've got to answer questions.'

'And if I don't?'

Flagg shrugged. 'That's easy enough to handle. I turn you over to the lawyers. They'll get you into court. But you know what that means. A waste of time. A lot of expense. And it all comes out in the long run. This way is easier. You give me answers to what I ask—and I forget what I don't need.'

She looked at him uncertainly. 'How do I know you will?'

'You've got to take a chance on it.'

She laughed a harsh, ragged laugh. 'That's a lot of help. Give me some more gin, Inspector. What about you?'

Newall refilled her glass. 'Not for us, Mrs. Bolton. We're on duty. If we went out of here with the smell of this rotgut on us we could never live it down. The policeman has to consider his reputation.'

Flagg sighed. 'That's true. Now, Mrs. Bolton—you got a job?'

She looked at him for a moment. 'Not now. I used to have one.'

'Who with? I want the name of the firm?'

She shook her head. 'Well, you won't get it.' There was a little smile in her pale eyes. 'I'll tell you this much. My boss was a very good friend of mine—and I was in a bit of trouble then. I'd just lost Bert—and things were pretty rocky. I was a nice-looking kid—believe it or not. He got quite fond of me.'

'So he put you in here?'

She nodded. 'Naturally it isn't the sort of thing you

152

like to talk about. A girl has got her pride. But there you go, that's the story. And don't ask me his name. I'm not telling you that. He's a fine, respectable man—and if I never see him now—he was good to me at one time. I wish him no harm.'

There was admiration in Flagg's gaze. 'That's nice of you. We'll get down to facts now, Mrs. Bolton. What do you know about Varney?'

'Very little. He's a friend of mine, but you don't know all your friends very well, do you? Not their private business, I mean.'

'What is his private business?'

'I don't know. He's never said anything about that. All I know is, he's got some sort of agency up north somewhere. He lives up there most of the time.'

'Up where?'

She was vague. 'I'm not really sure about that either. He talks a lot about Manchester and Newcastle and places like that—but I can't tell you any more.'

Flagg settled back. 'Suppose you tell me what you can then?'

She gave him a brief résumé of her acquaintanceship with Mr. Varney. She had met him by accident at a restaurant which she occasionally patronized near Sloane Square. They had become friendly and he occasionally called at the flat. She had seen him a week or ten days before and they'd spent an evening at a theatre. Afterwards he'd taken her out for late supper and they'd come back here for drinks. So far as she was concerned, the friendship with Sid Varney was open and above board. From what he had told her he had interests in the midlands and the north-east. He was a single man and lived at his club when he was in the north. When he was in London he lived at Clayton's Hotel in Beresford Road.

Flagg considered her thoughtfully. Was this true? Certainly she had spoken without any obvious attempt at dissimulation, and in substance her story could be very largely true. But while it might be true in parts, he was too old a campaigner to accept it all without further corroboration.

'Well, Mrs. Bolton, what you've told us has been a help. What we've got to do now is to have a talk with Mr. Varney and check it. Where do we find him?'

Eve Bolton stared at him. 'Find Mr. Varney? I can't tell you that. I don't know where to find him.' She saw him frown, then went on wildly: 'You don't believe me, Superintendent. That's the truth. I know he stays at Clayton's when he's here, but I can't tell you any more than that. When he comes to London he usually rings me up.'

'So that's all you can tell me about this fellow?'

'That's all I can tell you and if you keep me here talking for a month there's no more I can tell you.' There was a note of truth in her voice. Flagg surveyed her in silence for a moment.

'Fair enough. If it is—it is. I hope you're telling the truth. I'll get in touch with the Manchester Police at once. If Varney's in business in Manchester it won't take them long to find him. I hope for your sake, Mrs. Bolton, they do.'

She swallowed. 'I didn't say it was Manchester. I only said I thought it was. He talked about Manchester and Newcastle.'

'Did he ever say anything about Leeds and Sunderland? Or Workington and Stockton? Or maybe Sheffield and Middlesbrough?' There was heavy sarcasm in Flagg's voice.

She shook her head. 'If he did I didn't hear him. If you don't believe me—well, that's up to you. And now, Superintendent, I've told you all I can. I'm not feeling too well either. You can't get any more out of me if you wait till next week. Anyway, I want to lie down.'

Flagg rose abruptly. 'All right, Mrs. Bolton. If we've got all we can get out of you—there's no point in waiting.

I've got to see Varney as soon as I can. If you can tell me where to find him—tell me. It will count for you.'

'I've no idea where to find him.'

He stared at her for a minute. In some odd fashion he felt she was telling only the truth here—and it was a truth which puzzled him. He looked over towards Newall. 'All right, Know All. We'll get along.' He walked over to the door. 'Such a smell of cats.'

She said: 'You get used to it. I'm fond of animals, Superintendent.'

'I can see that,' Flagg said. 'But it's against the law. There's a Keeping of Pekinese Dogs in Tenements Act —1912, I think it was passed. Correct me if I'm wrong. You could get into a bother for that with the Sanitary.'

'I'll take a chance on the Sanitary,' Eve Bolton said. She opened the door for them. 'Good-bye, Superintendent. I'm sorry I wasn't able to help you more.'

'It's a pity,' Flagg said. 'We'll maybe be back. Quite likely we will in fact. Maybe you'll have remembered one or two things by then. Good day to you.'

The door closed behind them. She listened to the tramp of their feet on the stairs, then crossed to the window. A moment later and they appeared on the pavement in front of the building. She watched them climb into the large black car, then drive away. For no more than a moment she stood there, then she made her way over to the telephone, sat down in front of it and dialled a number. A moment passed, then a soft voice said, 'Hello, who's speaking?'

'This is Eve. You didn't tell me Mark was dead.' There was a little shiver in her voice. 'Why was that? I ought to have been told.'

He said sharply: 'It was in the papers. You could have seen it.'

'I never read the papers. Anyway, I've had the police

up here.' She heard him draw in his breath. 'And I don't like it. You'd better let me know what it's all about. You can't keep me in the dark and expect——'

'That's true.' His voice hardened. 'I'll come along as soon as I can manage. It won't be just now because I've got something else on hand. But I won't be any later than I can help. Say eight o'clock tonight. You'll be at home.'

'Yes,' she said. 'I'll be at home. I don't want to go out.'

'Good,' he said gently. The line went dead.

26

SUPERINTENDENT FLAGG headed for Central Office and the privacy and comfort of his own room. It was a large room and its standard of furnishings approached near luxury. There were certain evil-minded and jealous men who sneered disparagingly at this, and suggested that it was a more comfortable room than that of the Commissioner of Police himself. There were letters awaiting him here, and there were one or two interviews to arrange. This routine his disorderly soul loathed. He turned much of it over to Inspector Newall, then as the clock was chiming four, he rang for his constable clerk, peremptorily summoned from his home to cope with the exigencies of the moment. Poole came in mutinously.

'I hope you're not going to keep me long, Superintendent.'

'I'm going to keep you as long as I need you,' Flagg

said. He looked at the smooth-faced, white-collared man with distrust. 'So far as I can see, Poole, you've been kept long enough. I don't know why you ever joined the Force.'

'I couldn't get any other kind of job at the time,' Poole said frankly. 'It was just before the war. You know yourself what things were like then, Mr. Flagg. A fellow had to do the best he could. But I must say it's worse than I expected.'

'It'll get worse still,' Flagg said. 'Starting right now. You've never done a policeman's job in your life, Poole. While other men have patrolled the streets in all kinds of weather, chased burglars, fought bandits and done things like that, you've hung around Scotland Yard grousing about pay and no promotion. Well, here's your chance. I'm sending you out on a murder case.'

Poole was considerably put about. 'What's that, Mr. Flagg? You can't do that. I don't know a single thing about murders. I'm a police clerk pure and simple. I've never been anything else.' He shook his head in amusement at the preposterous notion that he should participate personally in a case. 'I'm not a detective.'

Flagg eyed him coldly. 'You've been promoted, Poole. Congratulations. You're going to Marchgate Priory with Russell, and you're going to keep your eyes open there for me. This is an important business, so watch you don't make a mess of it. It might affect my whole career. Get Russell up here.'

Russell made his appearance a few moments later, rested and refreshed. He had been on the 'phone to his wife, who had been considerably surprised to discover that he was in the Metropolitan area at all, and from her had received the intelligence that his in-laws had paid an unexpected Sunday visit.

'I'm damned glad I'm where I am,' he said. 'We gets that shower of vultures once a month. If I have to feed 'em, I don't have to listen to them. That's always something, Mr. Flagg. Now what's all this about Poole an' me going back to Marchgate.?'

Flagg told him briefly. 'You'd better go to the Knight Templar first of all. Get hold of Inspector Silver. I'll have him send a couple of men over to help you—but the heavy end of it will be on you and Poole. Especially Poole.' He looked at his clerk without pity. 'You, Poole, watch your step. This is a nasty job. Two men have been murdered already. I wouldn't like a man in my department to be the third. It would be a terrible disgrace and get me a bad name. I hope you've kept your insurance up-to-date and all your papers are in order.'

'This isn't funny, Mr. Flagg,' Poole said coldly. He took his departure.

Superintendent Flagg lit a large cigar. 'I should have gone myself,' he said sadly. 'But I'm needed here. Anyway, it's probably safer.' He took a sheet of paper out of his drawer and peered at it. For a moment or so he considered it, then looked across. 'Ever hear of Digby Branchman, Inspector?'

Newall looked surprised. 'Who was he?'

Flagg chuckled gently. 'He was a young C.A. when I was a young policeman. That wasn't yesterday. It's great how the time rolls on, Know All. Here I am——'

'What did this Digby Branchman do?'

Flagg scratched at his cheek. 'He had a line of his own—and made quite a packet out of it. In the end the law caught up with him. He didn't get much. He was a first offender, and a well-known and highly respected police officer went into the witness-box and put in a plea for him. He got off with nine months.'

'How much did he do in?'

'About two thousand if I remember rightly.'

'It paid him quite well,' Inspector Newall said.

Flagg sighed. 'You shouldn't say things like that. This here Branchman turned over a new leaf and reformed. You've heard about people doing that. Branchman did.

158

It pleased old Inspector Prosser more than anything else that ever happened to him in his whole career. He's dead now. In a way it's a good job.'

'Who is dead—Branchman?'

'No. Prosser,' Flagg said. 'He was a fine old man. One of the best policemen I ever worked under. He never hit a man in his life without asking for Divine guidance about it. We could do with more like him today.'

Newall was mystified. 'How does he come into it?'

Superintendent Flagg scratched at one side of his head. 'I think I know,' he said cautiously. 'But I'm not sure enough to talk about it yet.' He became suddenly brisk. 'How are you getting on with that report?'

'I'll be done in a quarter of an hour.'

'Good. Let me know when you're finished.' He sat back, put his feet up on the edge of his desk and closed his eyes. Inspector Newall toiled on uncomplainingly, and when his task had been completed he pushed the paper from him.

'There we are, Mr. Flagg. You'd better sign it.'

Flagg opened an eye peevishly. 'What's this? Sign what? This place is no better than a slave-camp. You no more than get started to think, than somebody's got to start to make you do something that breaks your train of thought.'

'I thought you were sleeping,' Newall admitted. 'It was my mistake.'

Flagg affixed his signature to the south-east corner of the sheet, without reading it. 'That's that. I want another man. Go and get Mackay for me.'

Mackay appeared a few moments later. He was a tall, rawboned Scot, and he took the chair Flagg pointed to with some interest. 'The inspector says you want me, Mr. Flagg.'

'That's right. I've got a job for the both of you.' He spoke for some moments and they listened with keen attention. When he had finished, Newall said:

'You think something is going to happen?'

'I don't say it will. I think it may. On a job like this you have to do your best to figure out what may happen. So far we haven't had much luck.'

'That's why you sent Poole and Russell back to Marchgate Priory?'

'It is,' Flagg said. 'I like to have a reliable man on the job. This is the place to do your detecting from, Know All. Everything at your hand. First-class help. Science and all the rest of it. One thing more, you'd better have arms of some sort. This character could be dangerous. If I'm right he's killed twice. He might try it again. That's one reason I want nothing to do with it myself. Fat men like me are too easy to hit. You young fellows are different. You can dodge and run.'

They left a little perplexed, and Superintendent Flagg rose, then made his way from the room. He went along a corridor, then down a stairway, halting at a door on which he knocked sharply. He turned the handle and went in.

An elderly man in a severe grey suit sat at a desk, a pen in his hand and an expression of some irritation on his rugged features. He said: 'Hullo, Flagg. Haven't seen you for an age. Have you come in for information, or a smoke, or what?'

Flagg laid a silver-wrapped cigar in front of Inspector MacPherson. 'Smell that, Mac.'

MacPherson lifted it up gingerly, even suspiciously. 'What is it?'

'A cigar. One of the best. You won't smoke another one like that in your life unless I give it to you. Keep it for your retiral if you like.'

MacPherson peeled off the wrappings to disclose a fat brown object of delight. 'So it is. Who would have thought it?' He produced a knife and cut the end off it before Flagg could ask for it back. 'Got a match?'

Flagg gave him a box. He struck one and put the box in his pocket. 'What is it you're after?'

Flagg said, 'You remember old Prosser, Mac?'

'I remember him well. The Devil's Own! We spent all our time putting away the hooks, and his hobby was getting them out again. A waste of good work.'

Flagg said: 'I see you're of the same mind as myself, Mac. Do you remember a case you worked on with him when you were a young detective? It had to do with somebody called Ostler, or Whistler, or a name like that. I wasn't in on it—but I remember the talk at the time. We took an accountant for it—name of Branchman— Digby Branchman. Old Prosser put in a good word for him and he got off with a matter of months.'

Inspector MacPherson puffed reminiscently. 'I remember it fine. Branchman was the chap. A nasty character he was. It was me that brought him in and he wanted to argue the toss because I'd forgotten to pick up a warrant when I left. I had to give him a skelp across the back of the neck before he saw I was in earnest, and he came along as quiet as pussy.'

Flagg sighed his pleasure. 'Did you ever hear what happened to him when he came out?'

'I think he went abroad,' MacPherson said. 'In fact I can remember old Prosser having him along to his meeting in that wee shed in Gowlock Lane before he went away. Prosser used to have all the thugs and old lags in the place there. He gave them free buns and cocoa, and they could always touch him for a bob or two. '

'You don't remember where he went?'

'Canada,' MacPherson said. 'I remember it fine. In those days all the ex-cons were going out to Canada.'

Flagg rubbed his hands together. 'I'm glad to hear you say that, Mac. I'm glad to hear about Branchman. Tell me anything you can remember about him.'

MacPherson did his best. For five or ten minutes he made Herculean demands upon his memory and at the the end of that time Flagg was content.

'I've never met him myself,' he admitted. 'But I hope to

do so, Mac. It's a small world we're living in too. It's a fine thing policemen have good memories. If we weren't always on the job, I don't know what would happen.' Flagg rose stiffly, then: 'It was you who picked up Branchman. You said he was nasty to take.'

MacPherson nodded grimly. 'He was. I remember it yet. If I hadn't been smart enough to belt him, I was for it. There was a paper knife on the desk and he grabbed it up. The pity is there was no one to see him. It was his word against mine and no more was said about it. But it taught me a lesson, Flagg. I never went after a man again unless I had a witness with me. You've got to watch your step.'

Flagg nodded. 'You're dead right. Well, if he was nasty then, he'll be nasty still.' He made his way back to his office. The telephone was ringing as he opened the door. He lifted the receiver.

'Hullo. Superintendent Flagg speaking.'

It was Rapley. He said: 'We've got hold of something here, Flagg. The boys have picked up a feller who saw a car arrive at Newsome Court this morning. The time doesn't fit too exactly, but it's close enough.'

'I'll come over,' Flagg said. He hung up quickly.

27

INSPECTOR RAPLEY was at Newsome Court when Flagg arrived, his feet stretched out towards an electric heater, and a large-bowled pipe in his mouth. 'We've made a pretty thorough check, Superintendent. Sergeant Brickner brought this feller in. I had a word with him and I figured you'd better see him for yourself. Then there's another man turned up—a bus driver. He's over at D.H.Q. just now. I've told them to bring him over.' He summoned a uniformed man through. 'Tell this feller Tillman we're ready to have a word with him now.'

Tillman was brought through a moment later. Rapley sat back, pointing his pipe at his colleague.

'This is Superintendent Flagg, Mr. Tillman. He wants to hear what you've got to say. The superintendent's in charge of the case.'

Tillman's story was straightforward. He lived in a similar block of flats on the opposite side of the street. This morning, however, he had been waiting for a friend who was to pick him up at ten o'clock and drive him to Esher. On the presumption that his friend would scarcely be up to time, he had prepared himself at his leisure and had gone through to the sitting-room to watch for the car, a few moments after ten o'clock. It had been almost ten-thirty when the friend had arrived. They had left at once. For twenty minutes he had been standing by the window and in that time two cars had halted in the immediate vicinity and he had watched both of them. One of the cars had stopped at least a hundred yards along the road. A couple had got out of it and gone into an adjacent house. The other car had halted almost across from him. It had been a small black car. A man had got out of it and had gone into No.34. He had been there for a very short time indeed for he had seen him reappear almost immediately. He had got into the car and had driven away almost at once.

Flagg said, 'At what time was this?'

Tillman thought it must have been at least a quarter after ten—probably even later by a moment or so. The car had no sooner disappeared than his own friend had arrived. When he had returned from Esher his wife had told him about the murder and he had come along voluntarily to offer his evidence for what it was worth.

163

'You saw the driver go into No. 34. Can you describe him?'

Tillman could not do so in any satisfactory fashion. So far as he could remember he was a man of average height. He had worn a rather long trench coat and a green soft hat which had been drawn well down over his forehead. It had not been possible to see the man's face.

Flagg thanked him and let him go. When he had gone Rapley looked at him gloomily. 'There you go, Flagg. That's what you have to put up with. He saw the murderer. He don't know any more about the car than it was a small black one, and about the man than he wore a long coat an' a green hat.'

'He's established the time,' Flagg said. 'He puts it at a quarter past ten. That knocks our other ideas on the head, Rapley.'

'It does,' Rapley said. 'By a quarter of an hour and maybe more. We've got to explain away that extra twenty minutes. As though we didn't have enough bother. Maley and that Mrs. What's-Her-Name both heard the shot, if it was a shot, a few minutes before ten.' He scowled at Flagg. 'Unless Hudson had had two visitors.'

Flagg chuckled softly. 'I don't think there's much doubt about that. Hudson had two visitors all right. The first one was the killer.'

'Then who was the second?'

'I've got half an idea,' Flagg said softly. 'What about your bus driver, Rapley?'

The bus driver had arrived and was brought in. He, at any rate, was under no misapprehension as to the make of a car.

'It was an Austin,' he said. 'An A-30—a black job. I saw her at the corner when I turned into Newsome Court.'

'Did you get the number?' Rapley asked briskly.

'No, sir, I didn't. It was because of the number plates I noticed the car. They were all splashed with mud and dirt so you couldn't read 'em at all. I was going to give

164

him a wave to tell 'im to get 'em wiped off before some long-nosed rozzer gave 'im a ticket for it.'

'Oh, you were, were you?' Rapley said.

'That's right, sir. They can get plastered up like that quite easy an' you don't think to get out an' look. That's the way you get into trouble.'

Flagg said, 'Did it look like a car that might be a city car or maybe one that had come in from the country?'

'From the country I would say. There ain't much mud and dirt in the City streets.'

'And the time?'

'Between ten-fifteen and ten-twenty. A minute or two either way, sir. An' that's all I can tell you.'

He left and Rapley peered over at Flagg. 'Does it help?'

Flagg sighed. 'We'll see. If that's all you've got here, Rapley, we'll go over to D.H.Q. and see what's come in.'

Inspector Rapley was in complete agreement. 'The sooner we get this business cleared up the better I'll like it.' On the way over to Divisional Headquarters he expounded his opinion. 'It looks very much like as if Hudson had these two callers. One at a few minutes before ten o'clock—and one shortly afterwards. The first was the murderer.'

'That's what I think,' Flagg said.

'You think Lew Hudson's death is linked with the Bentley murder?'

'I think it is,' Flagg said. 'It has to be.' He sat in silence till D.H.Q. was reached. Here, in Rapley's room, there was a considerable amount of material to be examined. For an hour and more he sat over it, his wire-rimmed spectacles high on the bridge of his nose. At six o'clock a turnkey brought in a pot of strong tea and they desisted from their labours to drink it. Inspector Rapley was in no forthgoing humour. He sat rather upright at his desk, a scowl on his heavy features.

'They don't make things any easier for you, Superintendent. This was supposed to be my day off too. I don't know how often it's worked out like that in the last thirty years. Did you get anything from the Bolton woman about this feller Varney, old Colling was talking about?'

'Not a great deal.'

Rapley was exasperated. 'Pity the poor policeman if he has to rely on outside help. It's a good job we've got our wits about us. What did she tell you?'

Flagg gave a brief account of the interview to which Rapley listened, frowning. 'It sounds fishy,' he said. 'I wish I'd seen her for myself. She sounds like a tart an' you know what to expect from that kind of piece. A widow you say?'

'A widow she says,' Flagg corrected.

'Maybe—an' maybe not. She didn't give you much about Varney?'

'Nothing at all—except that he comes from the midlands or the north. More than half the people in London come from the north. They all overstep themselves, Rapley. Even the clever ones. You wait long enough they always give you a chance.'

Rapley blinked. 'Are you talking about this Mrs. Bolton? What's so clever about the likes of her?'

Flagg rose. 'Quite a lot I figure. We'll soon see.' He drew on his coat. 'I'd better get back to Central Office. I've got a call to pay this evening and the sooner I get it over the better.' He went to the door. 'I'll ring you sometime this evening, Inspector. If anything crops up—let me know about it as soon as you can.'

'Trust me,' Rapley said. 'I wish you luck of it. I'm glad I'm not stuck with a job like that. That's always something to be thankful for.'

'It is,' Flagg said. He went out to the car that was waiting for him and climbed stiffly into the rear of it. For a moment or so he consulted a little notebook which he carried in his waiscoat pocket, then, to the solemn-faced young police driver who still waited his instructions: 'Clayton's Hotel,' he said. 'It's in Beresford Road, South Kensington.' He sat back in silence for the duration of the journey. It was vital that the mysterious Mr. Varney should be found—equally important that the link between Varney and Mark Bentley should be established, and that this might be a task of the utmost difficulty, he was well aware.

Half an hour's driving brought him to South Kensington and to Clayton's Hotel, a tall sedate-looking building of grey stone. He went up the three stone steps, pushed open the doorway and a man in livery came forward to greet him. 'Good evening, sir.'

Flagg said: 'It's all that. I'm a police officer. I'd like a word with the manager.' Ahead of him he saw a door with the word 'Manager' printed on it. He made his way towards it, the porter anticipating him by a scant moment or so. The manager made his appearance at once—a slim young man with dark eyes and an appearance of alertness. He held open the door of the room. 'Watney says you're a police officer?'

'Superintendent Flagg, Central Office,' Flagg said. He went in and sat down in the most comfortable chair he could see.

The manager was a shade perturbed. 'I've heard of you, Superintendent. By the way, I'm Mr. Hill. I hope there's nothing wrong. No complaints or anything of that sort. My board of directors are very particular and if——'

Flagg shook his head. 'Nothing like that at all.'

Mr. Hill relaxed a little. 'I'm glad of that, Superintendent.' He coughed. 'Can I get you a drink? If you——'

Flagg shook his head reluctantly. 'Not on duty, Mr. Hill. You know how it is. A public servant is a public servant. If somebody gets a smell of it off your breath, you're on the carpet.' He patted carelessly at his pockets, then looked up with an air of exasperation. 'Now isn't

167

that just devilish? Here I am away without my cigars. You wouldn't happen to have a cigar around the hotel any place? Most of the good hotels keep a few in stock.'

It transpired that Clayton's Hotel kept cigars for its more genteel patrons and Mr. Hill was pleased to produce a box. 'Help yourself, Mr. Flagg.'

Flagg's predatory intincts were aroused. 'Thank you, Mr. Hill. I'll take a couple just to keep me going. This being Sunday there are no shops open—it's a nuisance, but we have to put up with it.' He took two cigars and put them in his waistcoat pocket, then lit a third. For a moment or so he puffed contemplatively, then nodded. 'It's a good smoke. Well, let's get down to business. I've called round to make inquiries about a party who's been a guest at your hotel on several occasions, according to the information I've received.'

The manager's nervousness returned. 'I hope it's nothing serious, Superintendent. Nothing that might get the hotel a bad name.'

'It's serious enough,' Flagg said. 'In fact, it couldn't be any more serious. It's murder.'

'Who is he?'

'The name is Varney,' Flagg said. 'Sidney Varney. Now, Mr. Hill, you can do yourself, and us, quite a lot of good by telling us all you know about this man. When did you see Varney last?'

Hill licked his lips. 'Varney? No more than half an hour ago.'

Flagg stared at him in honest surprise. 'Half an hour ago?'

'Yes. He's a guest at present.'

There was a tense little silence. Flagg rose briskly. 'A guest, is he? Show me to his room.'

28

THEY went up together to a room on the second floor. Here the manager knocked on the door. There was no answer. He knocked again. There was still no reply and the man looked round. 'I think he must have gone out, Superintendent.'

Flagg tried the handle. The door was locked. 'Have you got a master key? I want to get in here.' He took the key the man handed to him. 'You might go down to the desk and find out if anyone saw him leave.'

Hill made his way downstairs. Flagg pushed open the door then stepped into the room. It was a large, square room, furnished with comfort, even luxury. In one corner of the room a small wooden frame had been built into the wall. It was occupied by a single green canvas bag. He lifted this, the better to examine it, but it was locked, and he was still looking at it when he heard Hill returning, a little out of breath from his exertions.

'Varney left the hotel just a few moments before you arrived, Mr. Flagg. Watney remembers seeing him leave quite clearly. He doesn't think it was any more than fifteen minutes before you appeared.'

Flagg swore softly. By so narrow a margin had he missed his quarry and complicated his own mission. 'When did he arrive?'

'About eleven o'clock this morning. He said he wanted to stay for a day or two.'

'Had he made a reservation?'

'No, indeed. Normally, he telephones us and does so. However this morning he arrived without having notified us. He told the receptionist he had had to make a hurried trip to London and wanted the room for a day or two.' He looked at Flagg unhappily. 'Now, Superintendent, what's all this about murder? I hope it won't affect the hotel because——'

'We'll talk about it in the office,' Flagg said. He led the way to it, but once ensconced in a comfortable chair seemed strangely loth to do so, and when Hill would have pursued the question, waved it aside ruthlessly. 'The first thing we have to do is to have a word with this porter who saw him.'

Watney was brought in to answer for himself. He had carried in Varney's bags from the car for him, and had waited by the desk while he had arranged for his room. He had taken him up to his room, and had seen him again briefly at lunch. The man must have returned to his room in the afternoon. Of this Watney could not be completely certain, but he had certainly seen him leave the hotel shortly before Flagg himself had arrived. 'Ten minutes or so, sir,' he said impressively. 'Not much more.'

'Could you describe him?'

Watney thought he could, and made a reasonable attempt at it. 'Pleasant enough looking gent, but a pretty hard eye in his head.' He went on to particularize and Flagg listened approvingly. When he had finished:

'You say he arrived in a car. Was it a private car or a cab?'

'A private car,' Watney said. 'A little Austin; a black one. Fair plastered with mud it was. Mr. Varney comes from the north somewhere and he probably drove hard all the way.'

Superintendent Flagg smiled. The mystery of the second visitor at Newsome Court was a mystery no longer. He dismissed the man, then: 'That's that, Mr. Hill. We'll do the best we can. I've got to get back to Central Office now. But if Varney returns, I want you to notify me at once.'

Hill was only too willing to promise to do so. 'I hope nothing in the way of trouble will come out of this, Superintendent. I don't want any fuss.'

170

'You and I think alike,' Flagg told him and went out to the waiting car. He drove back to New Scotland Yard with some haste, for there was one telephone call at least which he expected. It came shortly after he had returned and he settled back with satisfaction to hear the familiar voice of Poole.

'Is that you, Mr. Flagg?'

'It is,' Flagg said waspishly. 'I called you best part of an hour or so.'

'I was out,' Poole said. 'On the job. I don't think much of it. If I'd known there was something like this in the wind I'd have got dressed for it. The sort of light suit I've got on is no use for country wear—and I've been standing about in puddles of water with quite a light pair of shoes on. I'm sure I'm going to have an attack of 'flu again. You remember the last one I had and——'

'Stop talking about yourself,' Flagg snapped, 'and give me a report.'

'I was just coming to that,' Poole said sulkily. 'But I thought you would be interested in my impressions of the job, but of course if——'

'What about Marchgate Priory?'

'Everything is much about the same here. We're keeping an eye on him, of course. But it isn't easy, Mr. Flagg.'

'It never was,' Flagg said coldly. He spoke for a moment or so then hung up, confirmed in the comfortable knowledge that he had done all that was possible for him to do; that he had taken all precautions necessary in accordance with the information which was at his disposal.

The killer still walked abroad. He was unpleasantly conscious of that fact, and his dispositions had been made in the surety that he would strike again. If he were right in his calculations, there would be such an attempt. For half an hour more he sat smoking and at the end of that time the telephone rang again. This time it was

Inspector Newall reporting. 'Things are all quiet at this end, Mr. Flagg. What about you?'

'Varney's in London,' Flagg said softly. 'He booked in at Clayton's at eleven o'clock this morning. So far as I can make out he was there until a couple of hours ago. Now, he's on the loose. Keep your eyes open.'

'Trust me,' Newall said, then: 'What about the Marchgate end of it?'

'Poole reported half an hour ago. They've got half a dozen men in the vicinity. I think that's tidied up.'

'I hope so,' Newall said. 'I'll ring off now, Mr. Flagg. But as soon as there's a movement I'll buzz you. Keep close to the 'phone, for it may come in a hurry.' He hung up and Flagg sat back thoughtfully, a little glitter of interest in his shrewd eyes. He was poring over a buff-coloured sheet, covered with closely typed characters, when there was a tap at the door. 'Come in.'

Inspector Carmody came in. He stood in the doorway looking down. 'Well, well! The old maestro himself. I've got some information for you, Flagg. I've just come from ballistics. We got in the bullet they dug out of this fellow Hudson today. We've had it, and the bullet from Mark Bentley, under the comparison microscope.'

Flagg's eyes narrowed. 'And what was the result?'

'They were both fired from the same gun.'

Flagg sat without moving at all. Carmody looked at him anxiously. 'Is that good or bad?'

The big man chuckled. 'It's what I was expecting and what I was hoping for. The same gun killed Mark Bentley and Lew Hudson. That doesn't mean the same man killed him—but it means I'm getting warmer. Carmody, I wouldn't——'

The telephone rang out as he spoke. He lifted the receiver, then: 'Superintendent Flagg here.'

It was Newall who spoke. 'Car's arrived, Mr. Flagg. It halted about a hundred yards away and he walked up. He's there now.'

172

'Draw in on him,' Flagg said grimly. 'I'll be along right away.' He slammed the receiver down, elation in his heart, for a theory was proving itself to be true.

29

IT WAS the ringing of the door-bell which brought Eve Bolton from the kitchenette of her flat into the hall. For a second or so she stood beside the door, listening, indecision in her eyes, then: 'Who's there?'

Someone coughed. She heard a voice say, 'This is Varney.'

She hesitated no longer, but opened the door. She saw his rather thickset figure silhouetted against the lighter colour of the wall as she stood there. 'Come in, Mr. Varney. I'm glad to see you.'

Varney came inside. He wore a long trench coat which added to his height, a green hat which was drawn down over his eyes, and long leather driving-gloves. He followed her into the room and stood by the table looking around him.

She looked at him almost coyly. 'Aren't you going to take off your things?'

'Not tonight,' he said curtly.

She went across to close the door and as she did so he noticed that she staggered slightly. There was a newly opened gin bottle on the table, and the glass beside it showed traces of liquor in it. She went over to the table and began to pour out a glass. She carried it over towards him. 'I got your call, Sidney,' she said. 'From Slough. I've never known anyone from there.' She handed the

173

glass to him. 'I'm glad you called. I've been so upset all day. The police were here.'

He watched her impassively. 'Were they?'

'Two of them.' She sat down across from him. 'A man called Flagg. He said he was a superintendent or something. What does it mean?'

'Can't you guess?'

Her eyes were fixed on his. For just a second there was a faint little flicker in them, then she raised the glass, sipping it slowly. 'I suppose I can, Sid. I haven't many illusions left. You can't live the sort of life I've lived and have them. You've got to give up something. I never thought it was just me you were interested in. Not after the first week or so.'

He watched her with cold amusement. 'You didn't?'

She shook her head. 'No. I've had a bit too much experience of life for that. At one time you might have been interested in me. But not now. There was a time when I was quite a good-looking kid.' She laughed harshly.

He said, 'I don't find it hard to believe.' He leaned forward. 'I think it's about time you and I had a little talk, Eve.'

'About what?' There was cold suspicion in her voice.

'About a lot of things,' Varney said. He laid down the drink. 'What did Flagg want with you?'

'He wanted information. Mostly about you as far as I can judge. I was surprised it was you he was interested in. I thought it would be somebody else.' She finished her drink then went over to refill her glass. 'Drink up, Sid —I'll give you a refill.'

'Forget the booze for a while, Eve. You've been at the bottle all day. That's a bad sign. It's going for your nerves. The police know about you now. They'll keep on probing till they find out about it—all of it.'

There was a little flicker of fear in her eyes. 'It was you they were interested in. It wasn't me. If it hadn't been for you they wouldn't have been here yet.' Her fury had burned itself out as quickly as it had flared up. 'What do they want you for, Sid? You can tell me. I'm safe.'

He laughed a chill little laugh. 'Get it out of your head the police are interested in me, Eve. If they are it's only as a means to an end. I'm the means. You're only the road to the end.'

'What do you mean?'

Varney leaned towards her. 'I think it's time we had a little talk, Eve. I think it's time we understood each other.'

She looked at him over the edge of the glass. 'Well?'

He said: 'Mark is dead. He was murdered.'

For a long moment she sat there staring at him. The colour had gone from her cheeks and they were grey and ashen. 'You knew about Mark?'

Varney laughed mirthlessly. 'I knew about him.'

'What else did you know?'

'I knew he was your husband,' he said. 'But I didn't know until a very short time ago that he was still your husband until the day and hour of his death.'

She gave a little gasp. 'You know that? Who told you?'

'Nobody.' There was a mirthless smile in his eyes. 'You kept pretty quiet about it, Eve. Nobody suspected you were married. Nobody ever dreamed of it. Between you, you worked it pretty well, didn't you?' Ice dripped on the blade of his fury. 'Every story has its end, Eve. I think we're going to have the end of this one.'

She was staring at him stupidly. 'I—I don't understand you. I don't know what you're talking about. Get out of here. Get out or I'll call the police.'

He stood there looking down at her. 'The police? They'll be here soon enough. Do you think Flagg's a fool? My guess is he knows all he needs to know.' He leaned over her, his voice suddenly calmer. 'Eve, you've got a lot to answer for—but maybe you've suffered, too. You must have loved Mark at one time.'

She looked at him through bleary eyes. 'What if I did?'

175

'You've got one chance, Eve. One very thin chance of life!'

Behind him, someone laughed.

Varney swung round in an instant. He stared at the man who stood there in the doorway, stared at the silencer on the long barrel of the gun. It was held in a hand which was as steady as a rock.

'Verrall,' he said thinly.

Verrall took one step forward. 'That's right, Mr. Blane. It is Mr. Blane, isn't it? Mr. Blane of the Knight Templar?'

Peter Blane shrugged. 'That's only half the truth, Verrall.'

'And what's the other half?'

Blane said softly, 'Since we've got to this stage, Verrall, there's no reason why you shouldn't know.' There was a smouldering light in his grey eyes. 'Take your memory back a bit, Verrall. Back about twenty years. Maybe you'll remember that Faith Bentley had a husband. I'm the husband.'

'Tommy Osborne?' The cold voice was oddly startled. He took one step forward. 'Tommy Osborne?' He looked over at the woman. 'That should make you laugh, Eve. You were Mark's cast-off. Osborne was hers.' He lifted the gun just a fraction of an inch. 'All right, Osborne. I heard you tell Eve she had one chance—just one chance of life. You haven't even got that!'

Osborne was watching him steadily, almost calmly. There was death in Verrall's eyes, and he read it there as one may read the printed word; saw it in the hard set of the lips, the tensing of the jaw muscles. And as he saw it, he saw something else. The hand which crept round the open doorway to the electric switch. The fingers that tightened over it.

The lights went out!

Klop! Something sang through the air like an angry bee. Tommy Osborne crashed to the floor, then threw

176

himself forward in a grotesque hurdling dive. He collided with a moving figure, and as he grappled with it, his hands closed over the barrel of the gun and he laughed in triumph.

The lights went on again. There were four men standing in the open doorway, and one of them was large and overpoweringly fat. He said: 'Let him up, Osborne. If you choke the life out of him we'll have to run you for it next, and there's been enough killing on this case to last a lifetime.'

Tommy Osborne came slowly to his feet. He was breathing heavily and there was a little trickle of blood from his right ear. 'Nicked me!' he said briefly.

Flagg chuckled. 'Old habits die hard,' he growled. 'This character always resists arrest. Did it the first time we ever took him.'

Verrall was scrambling slowly to his feet. Osborne looked at him, then at the large figure of Superintendent Flagg. 'You know him, do you?'

'An old friend,' Flagg said. 'Mr. Digby Branchman, meet the company. We took Selwyn an hour ago at Marchgate Close.'

But Mr. Digby Branchman said never a word.

30

THERE was a meeting in the later hours of the night in Superintendent Flagg's comfortable room and Flagg, with a large cigar in his mouth, looked about him with the air of a feudal noble, conferring with his menials.

The assistant commissioner was there. Superintendent

Byfleet, an ancient crony, was there and beside him Inspector Rapley. Inspector Newall sat by the doorway, and at his hand Tommy Osborne. The hour was ten, the atmosphere was pleasant, even congenial, when Flagg said, 'I think I hear MacPherson now.'

The door opened as he spoke. MacPherson looked in. 'My, it's like a wake in here. Or maybe a sergeants' smoker.' He came in and, probing through a blue haze, found a chair.

Flagg said: 'Well, I'll run over it briefly, gentlemen. I'm not going to give you the details. You'll get them all in my report. Old Know All's started it already—but I'll give you the bare bones of it all.

'This thing started a long time ago, when the most of us here were younger and thinner and had a lot more teeth than we've got just now. And from the beginning it was simple blackmail, though in the end it became more than that.

'It begins with Mark Bentley. Bentley was a bit of a weakling, though as he grew older his character went through a radical change. Bentley himself was an orphan, but his father's brother was a Cyrus Bentley who made a killing on the Exchange during the First World War. A lot of people said he did it by rigging the market and there was some talk of an investigation though it didn't come off. That's got nothing to do with this case, but it does give you the background to it.

'Mark Bentley, then, was his uncle's heir—and he was very much under the old man's thumb. Old Cyrus kept him there and while Mark didn't like it, he had to put up with it, for the pickings were too good to lose.

'This case begins for us when Mark went out to Canada on a trip in 1937. In part, it was a business trip, and while he was on it, he met a man who called himself Stephen Verrall. Verrall was in reality Digby Branchman, a man who had already served a short sentence in this country for embezzling funds. He was an accountant,

178

and I've no doubt a pretty smart character. Whether he knew Mark or not, I don't know, but he certainly knew old Cyrus Bentley, and I think he saw that there was the chance of a lifetime here.

'Branchman introduced Mark to an English girl—Eve Bolton, who was living in Toronto at the time, and Eve had been prepared for her part of the job. It wasn't very difficult. In those days, Eve was an attractive girl and Mark, who'd been kept pretty much in hand, was a susceptible kind of fellow. Anyway, she tells me they were secretly married in less than a month after they met. They had to keep it that way, for old Cyrus would have cut Mark off if the truth had come out. Cyrus had his own plans and they had nothing to do with Eve Bolton.

'So far, things had worked out to suit Branchman. My own guess is he meant to work a simple squeeze on Mark Bentley for what he could get—but that was where fate stepped in and took over. Two things happened. The first was that old Cyrus Bentley had a heart attack and died, leaving his estate to Mark. The second and the most important was that within a matter of months afterwards, Mark Bentley had met Faith Osborne and had fallen in love with her.' He looked over at Osborne. 'That's right, Tommy?'

Osborne nodded. 'That's right, Superintendent. They met at some party and that was the start of it. I was in Berlin at the time. Faith wrote to me and asked me to divorce her.' He looked round them. 'From then on it wasn't very pleasant. I flew over to London as soon as I could—and I saw her twice. She refused to come back to me.' He was silent for a moment. 'Well—I gave her her divorce. Jane was only a baby at the time. She took Jane.'

Flagg said: 'There you go then. Mark Bentley waited till Faith Osborne had her divorce, then he married her. But he was a married man himself. He'd have given anything to have been able to get rid of Eve Bolton. But that wasn't possible. Eve had disappeared. Verrall took

179

care of that. From then on, Verrall took charge of his affairs, and he must have milked Mark for plenty. I don't know that we'll ever learn how much. Verrall became his adviser and his counsellor. He let people understand that he was his lawyer, but Verrall had never qualified in Law. I checked up on that after I came into it. Verrall, then, had all he needed. There was no need for any crude demands for money; no need to ask blackmail. Verrall was given a position of responsibility. Verrall was necessary to Mark Bentley, Verrall was the only person alive who knew about Eve Bolton, and Verrall kept her at a distance.' He looked round them all.

'Eve Bolton was the strength and weakness of the whole scheme. Mark Bentley was very much in love with his wife. He was completely devoted to her and his whole life was built up round her. At the back of his mind there was always the fear that she would learn about Eve—and he was afraid that if she did, she would leave him at once. Verrall probably played on this fear. And so it went on. Mark was content; Verrall was feathering his own nest and Eve was given enough to keep her in comfort. She tells me she's always been fond of drink and Verrall kept her well supplied with it. She was on to a good thing—and she knew it. She had no more love for Mark than he had for her and she was wise enough to know that so long as she kept out of his way, there was money in it for life.'

The assistant commissioner said, 'Then no more might have come out of it?'

Flagg nodded. 'That's right, Major. Only, in the end, Mark began to get a bit more difficult. Whether he ever found out that Verrall had tricked him all along, I don't know. I'm inclined to think he did. But he began to get suspicious—to think more about Eve and what she could do. Eve was living openly enough by this time in a flat in Chelsea, and I've had a talk with her. She was quite pliable, but she never at any time realized that Mark was such a wealthy man, or she might have been a bit more awkward. She was on easy street. Sometimes Mark himself visited her—though not very often. She had picked up one or two gentlemen friends.' He looked over at Osborne. 'Tommy here was one. My guess is that Mark led him there.'

Tommy Osborne nodded. 'That's right, Flagg.' He looked round them all. 'After the divorce went through I knocked about quite a bit—and then the war came along. After that I was out in Canada again. That filled in the years. I came back to England two years ago, then I began to wonder a bit about Jane. Not about Faith— she'd gone her way—but Jane was mine, too. They were living at Marchgate Priory and I went down to have a look round there. I saw her on horseback—I even spoke to her. She had no idea who I was. When I came back to London I began to think matters over. The Knight Templar was for sale. I didn't know anything about hotels, but I figured I could learn. I bought it. From then on, there was something in life to live for. Jane came around quite a lot. She grew very fond of me.' He dropped his voice. 'In the end I had to tell her.'

'And she told you about Mark and Faith?'

'She told me that Faith had been very trying and difficult. She told me Mark was worried about her. I began to wonder if their marriage was going to break up. Mark used to go up to town a bit. I followed him and that took me to Eve Bolton's flat. I began to wonder about that and I'll be frank with you, I thought at first it was an affair he was having. But it wasn't just an affair. I began to take an interest in Eve Bolton myself. It wasn't very hard to do that. I picked her up in a restaurant and we had one or two evenings together. Eve was fond of drink —but she couldn't carry it. When she had it—she talked.' He smiled grimly.

'The trouble was, she never said enough. Only enough to make me wonder about things. She told me she'd got

181

married when she was very young. She told me it had been abroad somewhere. She said she sometimes saw her husband even yet. That was when I began to get my own ideas about things and piece them together a bit. I suspected, but I didn't know. I began to keep an eye on Mark. I couldn't follow him to London just so easily, but I watched him while he was here.'

'And you 'phoned him?' Flagg said softly. 'You started to ring him up at the Close to get him jittery?'

Tommy nodded. 'I did. I don't know how you come to know about that, Flagg, because I never spoke to anyone other than Bentley. Only once, Jane answered the telephone—and I wondered if she recognized my voice.'

'She did,' Flagg said. 'Anyway, you tried to put the pressure on Bentley?'

'Yes. I had the idea there was a lot more to it than there appeared to be on the surface. It was Jane who let me know about that. Mark had a friend, Johnny Selwyn, who visited them occasionally. Jane told me that both her mother and Mark wanted her to marry Selwyn. Jane herself had no interest in him and looked on him as only a friend of Mark's. In any event, she had met a young Canadian doctor about a year earlier. MacLean was at sea—on a passenger liner, but when his ship was in port, he came to the Knight Templar and met Jane there. Moreover, all his letters were enclosed in an envelope and addressed to me, so that there would be no gossip locally about it.'

Superintendent Flagg looked round him, like a benevolent conjuror about to produce a large rabbit. 'Well, gentlemen, there you have the picture as it was a month ago. Only things were altering.' He leaned forward.

'From what I can gather, Mark was changing. He probably began to realize after a good many years that he'd been too soft. We'll never know exactly what aroused his suspicions—now. But something did. He began to make his own inquiries, and to do that, he hired a private detective—a fellow called Lew Hudson. This Hudson was quite a smart character. How much he found out, I don't know—but it was enough to harden Mark's suspicions. The time for a showdown was nearer at hand than they knew.'

'What do you mean by that, Flagg?' Superintendent Byfleet looked over with curiosity.

Flagg said: 'Mark wasn't the only one who was suspicious. Verrall was leery himself. He'd been pretty much in Mark's confidence over the years. Probably he noticed the difference in his attitude. Anyway, Verrall saw the change and knew they'd reached a climax. Some day, there was going to be a reckoning. There was a choice open to him. Either he could clear off with what he'd got out of it—or he could stay where he was and play it his own way. I don't think he ever hesitated over his choice. There was too much money at stake. Too much to lose—too much to walk out on. Besides, he liked the sort of life he had. Why change it?

'Mark was getting dangerous. If Mark died, his fortune went to his wife and stepdaughter. Verrall began to look about for a suitable husband for Jane—and the man he chose was Selwyn whom I've already mentioned to you. Verrall had known him for years and Selwyn tells me he'd owed Verrall money over a long period of time. Selwyn claims that at the beginning he did not realize that murder was in Verrall's mind—and I think this is true. Moreover, I think murder was probably not even in Verrall's own mind at the beginning. My idea is that Verrall figured he was preparing the ground for the future and that with Jane married to Selwyn, he would have another pliant and easily worked character at hand.

'Only it didn't work out like that. Mark got suspicious —and dangerous. Verrall had tried to push Selwyn too openly and Mark began to smell a rat. He liked Selwyn and at first had been quite in favour of the match. Later

183

on, he changed his mind about it. The queer thing is that Faith Bentley approved of it. She liked Selwyn—and she wanted Jane to marry him.' He spread out his hands. 'That brings us up to the night of the murder. You've got the background—or as much of it as I can piece together. I don't say I'm right in every detail, and there's a lot of it we'll never know. But what you've got is close enough to the truth to let you understand the rest of it. And the rest of it began on Friday night.

'Mark had been worried about these 'phone calls. He brought Lew Hudson down to Marchgate Priory to see what he could do about it. Hudson came down on the morning of Friday and put up at the Knight Templar, where he called himself Warren—John Warren of Cheam Road, Brockley. Am I right, Tommy?' He looked to where Osborne sat.

Tommy Osborne nodded. 'You are. He came in at ten o'clock calling himself Warren, but in the boot of his car there was a part of an old petrol bill made out to Lew Hudson. I saw it when I was cleaning the car up. After that I had a look through his room while he was at lunch. He had a report written out in his case—it was a big help to me.' He laughed softly. 'It didn't tell me much I didn't know, but it did confirm what I had only suspected. After that, I kept my eye on him.'

'Tell them about the murder,' Flagg said softly.

Osborne leaned forward. 'I told you I'd been watching Hudson. That afternoon he put through a call to the Close from the house 'phone. There was no one about and I suppose he figured he was safe enough for a short call. Anyway he told Bentley he had something important to tell him and they arranged to meet at the East Lodge at seven o'clock that night. I heard the call on my own 'phone in my office and I was at the East Lodge myself at about a quarter to seven. I moved into the bushes beneath the windows and waited. Bentley came along a few moments later. He went out to the gates—then to the

184

road. After that he came back and I heard him speak to someone.'

'Verrall?'

'It was Verrall,' Osborne said. 'But I didn't know that at the time—nor did Mark. Bentley led him into the house. A moment later I heard him call out—"It was you!" After that there was a single shot.'

'What happened then?'

'Verrall came out and ran back up the driveway towards the Close. He passed quite close to me. When he had gone I ran inside. Mark was dead. I came out again and I could hear Verrall running in the avenue. I was standing there when I heard a car engine and a light came round the bend. I figured it was Lew Hudson arriving. I decided to go after the killer, and I caught up with him before he reached the house. He was breathing pretty hard by that time, but he cut across the lawn towards the study, and went in by the window. It was Verrall without a doubt.'

'There you go,' Flagg said. He looked around. 'A cool character. He'd made up his mind Bentley had to go. This was the chance. If he'd waited any longer, Mark might have done something about it. Verrall must have been watching him. He must have known Bentley had gone to Hudson for help. A man so clever as Verrall was, wouldn't be likely to slip up there. Anyway, you've heard the evidence. So far as we can see, Verrall sat in the study with Bentley, talking as nice as you like and having a drink with him. When Bentley left, Verrall put a gun in his pocket and left, too. He must have followed him right to the East Lodge. When he got there, he knew this had to be it. Mark was up to something. Whether he knew he was meeting Hudson or not doesn't matter. Verrall shot him and went back to the Close. He must have managed to get in a word with Selwyn. They covered up for each other for the few odd moments that they might have to account for.'

185

'Remarkable,' said Byfleet.

'Remarkably simple,' Flagg said.

Rapley said impatiently, 'What about Lew Hudson?'

Flagg sighed. 'I'm coming to that, Inspector. On the Sunday morning we went up to the Close to question Clancy, because he had a bit of interesting information about him.'

'What was that?'

'I'd sent away one or two glasses,' Flagg said softly. 'Fingerprints sent me a report. Clancy had a record. I went up to question him. That was when I heard first about Hudson. Clancy told me. When we left, Johnny Selwyn was at the door of the room. At the time I wondered if he'd been listening.'

'Eavesdropping?' the assistant commissioner asked.

'Eavesdropping,' Flagg said. 'And he was. Clancy told me about Lew Hudson. At the time I didn't connect him with Warren, who'd been at the hotel, but later on I came to see he was the same fellow. Anyway, we drove straight to London to interview Hudson. When we found him he was dead.'

'That's right,' Rapley said. He thought for a moment. 'You said that Lew Hudson turned up at the Lodge when you were leaving, Osborne. He should have given the alarm.' There was proper indignation in his voice.

Flagg chuckled. 'My guess is he was afraid to say anything. I think he went in, found Bentley and drove back to the Knight Templar. Since nobody knew his interest in it, he probably figured the best thing to do was to sheer off, and say nothing. He did that. And next morning, Verrall rang him up just as soon as Johnny Selwyn had told him what he had heard. Verrall probably said he was Bentley's lawyer and he was coming round to speak to him.

'Hudson couldn't have been afraid of him. He opened the door for him, in his pyjamas and dressing-gown—and

186

they sat down to talk. Verrall just drew his gun and shot him dead.'

'The murdering devil,' Rapley said. 'It spoiled my Sunday.'

Flagg said: 'Half an hour later, Tommy Osborne had turned up—but that's neither here nor there. The death of Hudson put the finger on Selwyn. If he'd been a smarter man he wouldn't have done it like that. I sent Russell and Poole down to keep an eye on Selwyn, and I told them I wanted him picked up when I gave the word.'

There was a little silence. He took the cigar out of his mouth and blew a vast cloud of smoke into the air. 'That's all.'

Nobody spoke for a moment, then MacPherson said: 'You came down in the afternoon to ask me about Digby Branchman. How did you know that Verrall was Branchman?'

Flagg chuckled. ' "The evil that men do lives after them",' he said. 'That's literature. You ask old Know All here. What happened was that I got the break every good policeman deserves to get—and I got it because I worked for it. I told you I got Clancy's prints off a whisky glass. That was true. But I sent away three whisky glasses. The one Clancy had used—and the one that Verrall and Mark Bentley had used. The report I got back was that Clancy's prints were on record. I'd expected that. What I didn't expect was that one of the other sets of prints were on record, too. They belonged to Digby Branchman, an accountant who'd served a spell in this country for embezzlement as I've told you. I remembered Branchman. I remembered a bit of a controversy about him. He was a kind of a prize exhibit of old Inspector Prosser. I'd never seen him, but I remember the talk about him and I remembered, too, that Inspector MacPherson had been on the case—so I had a quiet word with him about Branchman. It helped.'

He sat back. 'That's all. Maybe there's one or two

loose ends to tidy up just for the book, but they'll be smoothed out.' He looked over at Tommy Osborne. 'What about you, Tommy? What do you mean to do?'

Tommy Osborne said quietly: 'I'm going back to Marchgate Priory. It seems that after a lapse of twenty years I've still got a wife on my hands.'

'And a daughter,' Flagg said. 'I hope you can do something about it. You're a young man yet. Younger than me even—and that's not bad if I say it myself. You've got a lot of life to live yet. Make the best of it.'

'I think you've got something there, Superintendent,' Tommy Osborne said. He smiled all round him. Somehow he had the idea that life was going to be different for him in the future. It was.